Play With Me

ANNA KATMORE

To Georgia Lyn Hunter,
the most supportive friend and critique partner
I could wish for.
Thanks for watching my back.

Play With Me

Chapter 1

He'd never tried to kiss me, even when we practically shared the same bed for half of the summer. And then he was gone. For five tormenting weeks. I thought I was going to die after day two.

But today, my torture was over. Today, Anthony Mitchell returned. My best friend and future husband.

Not like I had informed him of that yet, but it wasn't necessary. Everyone knew it, and I couldn't wait to trade my last name, Matthews, for his. Tony and I had been hanging out since kindergarten. We were inseparable, except for the few hours every day when he had soccer training and I had—well, some time to write how much I loved him in my diary for the sixteen millionth time.

Lisa and Tony, that went together like Bonnie & Clyde. Like Lois & Clark. We were M&M, really.

The door bell chimed.

My heart banged against my throat as I tossed my diary to the side, struggling to disentangle the quilt from around my legs. I finally flopped off the bed together with the comforter.

"I'm coming!" On the way down the winding stairs, I raked my fingers through my long, brown hair to give it the last bit of oomph before I rushed to open the door. A sunbeam hit me first, then Tony's long-missed good looks followed. His tousled blond hair fell over his forehead, almost touching his pretty blue eyes. He wore a white shirt half open, and I always had to fight really hard not to drool over his naked skin.

Hands shoved into the pockets of his shorts, he just stood there and looked at me. Then his mouth curled into his typical sly grin. "What is it, Liz? I know you're dying to hug me."

I flashed my teeth, which now were perfectly

straight after wearing braces for two years, into a broad smile and gave him the bear hug he expected. He dragged me outside and twirled me under the warm sun with my face buried in the crook of his neck. Ah, he smelled so good, sun-kissed and all Tony. I never got enough of that special brand.

"How was camp?" I asked after he set me down.

He mocked me by wrinkling his nose. "Boring as hell without you."

"Yeah, right. As if."

To fully understand him, one had to know that, apart from cheese crackers with mayo, soccer was Tony's greatest passion in the world. But I appreciated his lie and stuck my tongue out at him.

Tony tsked. "Manners, girl. If you want to kiss me, just say so." His face was close enough that his nose brushed mine. I swallowed the urge to tilt my head and do just that. But I knew he was teasing me again. So far, we'd never kissed. In regular intervals, I fell asleep in his bedroom when we played video games, or he would crash at mine when his parents were on business trips around the state. He let me rest my head on his shoulder, even played absently with my hair. But a kiss? Nah.

I was going to be seventeen at the end of this

summer and had started feeling a little weird because I hadn't been kissed yet. But no one other than Tony would touch my lips, and if he needed a few more months to realize he wanted me, too, I could wait.

"Hey, want to go down to the beach? I got this pretty new swimsuit and haven't tried it out yet." In anticipation of our reunion, I had put on the neon green bikini that morning, and now pulled down the collar of my pink tee to tease him with a glimpse. Green was his favorite color.

He snarled like a jaguar, with one corner of his mouth lifted. "I'd love to see you half-naked, Matthews." Just another tease, but it didn't matter. Goose bumps shot up on my skin. "Unfortunately, I have to pass. I'm going to see some friends from the team down at Charlie's."

My shoulders slumped. "Seriously? You just got back, what, ten minutes ago? Didn't you see the guys enough at camp?"

"Hunter wants to discuss tomorrow's tryouts."

I pouted. Ever since Ryan Hunter had become the new captain of Grover Beach's high school soccer team, Tony's training time had doubled. And more training meant less time for him to hang out with me. I hated Hunter.

"Cheer up, girl. Why don't you come along? You know most of the guys anyway, and I'll introduce you to the rest. I'm sure Hunter won't mind." He gave me no chance to argue, or even trade my flip-flops for decent shoes. My hand in a tight grip, he hauled me down the path through our front yard.

"Wait! I have no money on me."

"Don't need it. That single soda you'll sip on for the next two hours won't ruin me."

I pulled my hair back and fastened it with a hair tie I had in my pocket as we ambled along Saratoga Avenue to Charlie's Café and Diner.

A bunch of kids sat around three tables in the shade of the wooden roof sloping over half of the outdoor area. I recognized a few of them from Tony's team. Sasha Torres, Stephan Jones, Alex Winter. Nick Andrews' arm was laid in a cast. The training camp obviously hadn't passed without leaving battle scars.

I was surprised by the many female faces there, though. "What's this?" I whispered to Tony when we were still out of earshot. "Are you into co-ed training now?"

"Cool, isn't it? We played a few games together in Santa Monica, and Hunter thought it would be fun to assemble a mixed team here, too."

Some of the girls looked familiar, and I even had Spanish with Susan Miller. But a handful of them I swore I had never seen before. Like the one who stood as we approached and kissed Tony on the cheek with her awfully bright-red-painted lips.

"You're late, Anthony. I almost thought you wouldn't come."

Anthony? The only person I ever heard calling him that was his grandma.

"Hi, Chloe," he replied in a strange, deep voice I'd never heard before. His hands rested on her hips. He dipped his head and let her kiss his other cheek.

She winked at him then gave me the strangest once-over I ever got. The spite in her eyes made me feel as if I fell short in the looks and fashion department in her book.

My glance skated to Tony's face. *What the hell was that?* And seriously, he didn't have to drool over her shamelessly long legs when she sat down again and swung one over the other. Her white mini dress must have shrunk in the wash, because something red flashed underneath.

Tony shouted our order to Charlie behind the bar. A Coke and a Red Bull. The Red Bull certainly wasn't for me. But when did Tony start drinking that nasty stuff? Red-lips-and-white-dress had a bottle of that in front of her, too. I started feeling really awkward all of a sudden.

"Mixed soccer teams, huh?" I grumbled at Tony while we sat down—he opposite Chloe, and I between him and Nick with the cast.

"The tryouts are tomorrow, Matthews. I can put you on the list, if you're interested," Ryan Hunter called out to me, a mocking glint in his deep brown eyes.

The fact he even knew my name caught me off guard.

"Liz and soccer?" Tony laughed next to me. It hurt in a weird way. "You might as well try to get an elephant to dance the tango. Right, Liz?"

I directed an irritated scowl at my supposed best friend. He didn't even notice when the entire bunch joined in on the laugh.

"The elephant part hits home," Barbie said to the redhead next to her then flashed me a cruel smile.

Sorry, what? I was a perfect size XS. My five-feet-four might seem a little short to her Amazonian six-foot-something, but I was in no way fat. I picked up my dropped stomach from the ground and decided to punish Tony later for pretending not to have heard that. In all the time we had been friends, not once had he let anyone insult me without breaking their jaw. Okay, messing with Chloe's face would be a little drastic, but he could at least have said something to defend me.

Since he seemed to have forgotten how, I returned the saccharin-sweet smile to the Barbie clone. "I tried puking up my meals in ninth grade, but that seems to be more your thing than mine."

The laughter died, and Tony choked on his swig of Red Bull while the rest of the group pretended to be conversing in lowered voices. The only sound, a chuckle, came from the place where Ryan Hunter sat.

Chloe frowned at me as if I'd spoken a foreign language. "Did you just insult me?"

The funny thing was she really meant it. I cut a glance skyward and sipped on my Coke.

Thankfully, Tony got a text message from his mother not long after that. Mrs. Mitchell was hoping to see him again before she and her husband had to leave town for two days. Tony looked at my glass of soda and asked me if I wanted to stay with the others.

I downed the drink in three seconds, already standing. "Nope, I'm ready."

He shook his head, but smiled, and let me walk in

front of him.

"See you tomorrow, Anthony," Barbie cooed.

I ignored the rising heat of jealousy and resisted the urge to glare at her over my shoulder. Instead, I counted the tiles on the floor to the exit. *One, two, three…*

"How about it, Matthews?" Ryan Hunter said as I passed him. "Will you try out for the team or not?"

I stopped, stunned that he was serious about it. My eyes fastened on the easy smile he cast me. "I—"

Tony's hands on my shoulders gently pushed me forward. "You shouldn't tease her. She's just not made for soccer."

My heels dug into the ground. Not because he'd tried to save me from answering, but because of *her* snortling laugh behind me. "Know what?" I turned to face Tony with a determined glare. "I think I'll just give it a shot."

"You're shitting me."

That didn't require a reply, but I raised my brows at him anyway.

"Cool, so you're on the list. We meet at ten on the field."

I turned to Hunter's amused tone and gave him a polite smile. "I'll be there."

A ball cap shadowed his face as he lowered his chin, but I could feel his gaze skim down to where my cut-off jeans ended then travel slowly farther down my naked legs and back up. "Bring shoes." He smirked and winked at me.

This sent a shiver skating down my neck. Tony shoved me out of the café before I could figure out why.

We walked most of the way in silence, until we were close to home and I exploded right in his face. "I can't believe you did that!"

"What?" He looked at me, baffled, like a toddler who was robbed of his sucker.

"You let that girl insult me and didn't say anything."

"You had everything under control. And she didn't really insult you."

"Oh, right. *You* did! You called me an elephant."

Tony took my hand and pulled me with him. "You know it wasn't meant like that. I don't see why you're throwing a fit now. You've never liked soccer. When did that change?"

"Today. Now I *love* it."

"Yeah, I can see that. So badly that you want to be a player." He rolled his eyes. "Please, tell me you're not doing this because of Chloe."

I'm doing it for you, idiot. But it would have taken more than a crazy afternoon to tell him that. I gritted my teeth. "That girl can get lost in her closet full of Barbie dresses."

Suddenly, his arm was wrapped around my shoulders, and he pulled me close to his side as we walked on. "If I didn't know any better, I'd say you're jealous of her."

"We've been best friends since we grew out of our diapers," I moaned, slightly comforted by his embrace.

"And I promise we'll still be when we need them again." His laugh rocked me with him. "Chloe is just a girl who likes to play soccer. But you're the only girl I know who can watch *E.T.* without bursting in tears."

Even though there was an obvious note of admiration, I couldn't help but feel a chill sneak around my heart at the way he said it. Like I was one of the guys and not a *delicate girl like Chloe.* I wiggled out of his embrace, and a snort escaped me.

Tony quirked his brows. "What?"

"Nothing."

"Are you mad at me?"

"No," I grumbled.

He waited a second, eying me with skepticism. "O*kay*. Is this one of those moments where you say *no* but actually mean *yes?*"

Another growl. "No."

He slapped his hands to his face then slowly dragged them down, glancing helplessly at the sky. "You know I don't speak this language. Just tell me your problem."

"There is no problem!" I ran up the path to my house, slamming the door behind me.

Chapter 2

At nine thirty the following morning, I answered the door and found Tony outside. Hands braced on the doorframe and head hanging, he cast me a sheepish grin as he looked at me from under those incredibly gorgeous lashes.

"Still mad?"

I swallowed. The endless speech I had prepared for him the previous evening—including words like ignorant, idiot, and dumbass—slipped from my mind. "Never again call me an elephant," was all that came out in a low grumble.

"Promise." The silly boy pouted and even crossed his heart.

I smiled. "We're good then."

Tony's metallic green mountain bike leaned against our low picket fence. I grabbed mine from the shed, and we cycled to the high school soccer field together. Close to fifty girls and boys from tenth to twelfth grade had gathered in front of one of the goal posts. Someone was handing out numbers as we joined them. Already a member of the team, Tony didn't have to participate in the tryouts. But I lined up to get mine.

"Forty-seven…Matthews," Ryan Hunter shouted to Susan Miller, who wrote down names on a list. He gave me the sticker, which I was supposed to pop on my chest, and smiled. So far, I hadn't seen Ryan without his ball cap, except on rare occasions, and then from far away, too. But today, the sun played in his dark hair that fell devilishly over his forehead, giving him a whole new appearance. His unexpected good looks took me unaware, and he caught me staring. His matter-of-fact tone changed to a sly rumble. "Good luck, Matthews."

When everyone got their numbers, he raised his voice over the chatting crowd. "Okay, everybody. For a little warm-up, I want you to run three laps around the field then come back here."

Panic kicked me in the gut. "Is he kidding? Three laps?"

"Don't say you already regret going for the team."

I hated Tony's *I-told-you-so* chuckle as he dragged me from the trimmed lawn and started jogging next to me. Swallowing my retort, I tried to match his pace—impossible, of course, when one of his strides measured two of mine.

Shit, one lap seemed like ten miles. Screw Hunter and his warm-up. By the time I was done, I collapsed on the grass, hearing nothing but my own erratic breathing. Thank the Lord I had a chance to catch my breath as forty-six candidates attempted to score goals before it was my turn.

Tony got me a drink from the water cooler while I mimicked a dead frog for several minutes. My mouth and throat felt like the desert. As he stepped over me, his shadow was a welcome respite from the sun. I sat up, longing for the cup of water he held out to me.

But when I grabbed the plastic cup, my heart sank. "So little?" I held the mouthful of liquid against the sun, turning it this way and that, seeing if it would miraculously become more. "There's something seriously wrong with your head."

"Not at all." He laughed. "But since you can hardly breathe after this short run, more water would make you sick. In fact, it would be better if you just rinsed your mouth with this and spit it out."

I offered him a sneer. "Can I spit it into your face?" Not waiting for his comeback, I downed the little water he granted me. The sip evaporated on my tongue in an instant.

"Matthews! Your turn!" That was Hunter, and when I turned in his direction, the soccer ball came flying toward me. Praise my mad reflexes! I caught it before it hit my churning stomach. Tony pulled me to my feet and gave me quick instructions on how to hit the ball for the best impact.

Yeah, right. As if I really wanted to know that. I placed the ball on the ground then kicked it toward Frederickson who stood in the goal. It dropped to the lawn several feet in front of him then rolled on as if out for a relaxing stroll before it touched his left shoe.

My beam at Tony was full of fake enthusiasm. "Hey, what do you know, I got the direction right."

"Come on, Matthews." Ryan came jogging toward me with the ball under his arm. "I've seen you kick Mitchell's butt harder than that."

Beaten and exhausted, I was ready to surrender, but when he offered me the soccer ball, his lips curved into a mocking smile, which prompted me to prove him wrong. I accepted the challenge.

He planted the ball in front of me, but then he had me take several steps back. "Now take a short run and put a little more power in your thrust."

"Ah no, don't let him make me do that," I begged Tony, grabbing his shirt in growing horror. "We both know I'll just trip over the damn thing."

The boys laughed, and Tony pried my fingers loose from his collar. "No, you won't. Tell you what, if you hit Frederickson straight in the chest, I'll buy you a chocolate decadence ice cream sundae. Deal?"

Ice cream? If there was the right incentive... "Deal." I started forward and kicked hard, aiming for the redhead guarding the net. The soccer ball dropped neatly in Frederickson's arms.

"Well done!" Ryan told me. Then he sprinted back to the low desk where Susan took her notes and called Cynthia Ramirez to try her luck.

Unspeakably proud, I turned a smiling face at Tony. But my smile got lost the moment I glimpsed Barbie girl standing with him.

Hands laced behind her back, she rocked on her heels in front of him. Her boobs pushed out so far, she could have staked him in the heart. "Will you be at Hunter's party later?" she asked him in a sickly sweet voice.

I gulped. Ryan Hunter's parties were legend. I could only rely on the gossip in school of course, but rumor had it his father was friends with Chief Berkley, and so Ryan could turn up the music to a maximum all night. Beer flowed in endless rivers, and he even had his own pool table. The closest I had been to his house was when we drove by to get to the library, but it looked big enough to bear *several* halls. Getting an invitation to one of those parties meant stepping up into the *cool league*.

Not that I cared about hanging out with jerks like Chloe—yuck. But Tony had been to many of his parties, and he never told me much about the events behind those doors. That alone sharpened my curiosity.

He would go tonight for sure. The fact the Barbie clone would be there too had my heart slipping to my pants. I put up a nonchalant face while I actually felt like bawling and trudged over to the water cooler to get a drink larger than the fly pee Tony had brought me after the warm-up.

The afternoon dragged on with more exercises that involved passing the ball back and forth, zigzagging over the field with short kicks, and finally a count of how many times one could juggle the ball in the air without losing it. I got an amazing two and a half.

This was it. I was done with soccer. May the ball rot in hell and the players die of thirst. I didn't give a damn if I made the team or not. Playing ball in the scorching sun was for morons anyway.

I wiped the sweat off my face with the towel Tony had brought, then stuffed it back into his backpack, and stomped off.

"Hey, where do you think you're going?"

"Home."

Tony caught up with me. "You can't. Ryan hasn't announced the new players yet."

"Like I care."

He wrapped his arm around my shoulders and used my speed to propel me in the opposite direction. "You don't want to know if you're on the team?"

Trying to wiggle from him, I gave him a hard stare. "Nope."

"Where's your spirit gone?"

"Where has your *eyesight* gone?" I stopped dead. "You saw what a miserable player I am."

"Ah, I've seen worse. Actually, I'm pretty proud of you. This was the first time you came into contact with a soccer ball and you almost got a goal on the second try. All you need is a little training."

I found that hard to believe, but the expression in his eyes told me differently. He meant it. Confused, I gave him a sideways glance. Unfortunately, Chloe intruded into my view as she came skipping over to us like the tooth fairy. Her perfectly manicured fingers wrapped around his biceps as she bounced up and down before him.

"Come, quick. Hunter's naming the players in a minute. He already told me that I was on the team."

"I'm not surprised." Tony allowed her to drag him away from me. "You proved in camp you're a natural at soccer."

"Only at soccer?" She winked at him and skipped away.

My molars suffered from the hard grinding I did. The thing was—I needed to become a member of this team, badly. How else could I fend off this bimbo?

Ryan Hunter held a list in his hands as he stepped in front of the expectant crowd. "We need eleven new players. I'll call out the names of those who made it onto the team. If yours is among them, well done. If not, I'm sorry but hope you'll try again next year. You've all shown great enthusiasm today." He cleared his throat and reeled off the new players. "Stevenson. Jones. Summers—"

Since Barbie jumped with her friend then, I figured I now knew her last name.

"—Smith. Jackson. Daniels. Hollister. McNeal. Miller. Matthews. And Warren."

My jaw hit the dirt. I pivoted to Tony. "Did he just say Matthews?"

"Guess he did." His silly grin made me want to slap some seriousness into his face.

"I'm going to play?"

"Yes," he chuckled. "Now get your things, I owe you a sundae."

I really made it, *and* he owed me ice cream. What a freaking fantastic day. I jogged to the bench and slung my backpack over one shoulder. Certainly, I had the most stupid grin in the world pasted on my lips. It slipped as the word *owe* got stuck on repeat in my mind. What if he had asked Ryan to let me onto the team even if I was a miserable player? At the thought of depending on Hunter's mercy, I felt awfully embarrassed.

I had to know, and Tony would spill—even if it meant I had to threaten to crunch his entire six months' supply of cheese crackers, which he kept hidden under his bed.

Whipping around, I bumped into Ryan.

"Congrats, Matthews," he cheered. "You handled the tryout quite well."

"Yeah, whatever." Pissed at something I didn't yet have proof of, I shoved past him but then stopped. "What does Tony owe you for putting me on the team?"

For a moment, he looked confused. Then he laughed out loud. "You don't want to know."

My hands fisted around the strap of my backpack. Hell, of course I wanted to know.

Turning to leave, he glanced at me over his shoulder. His eyes sparked with a glint of mischief. "See you at my house, Matthews."

Holy shit. Did he just invite me to his party?

Chapter 3

The sundae was yummy, but so was Tony as he licked vanilla ice cream off his spoon. I couldn't take my eyes off his lips the entire hour we sat at Charlie's. Unfortunately, the boy was like a fortress. Bolted down. He refused to tell me what he had to give Ryan for letting me play on the team. Well, he actually said he didn't owe Hunter anything, but I didn't buy it.

At eight thirty that evening, Tony picked me up at my door and drove us to Ryan's house in his mother's car. I had no idea what people wore to those parties, but since it was still over sixty degrees in the evening—not unusual for Northern California in August—I chose a dark gray tank top and black hot pants. Judging by the smirk I earned from Tony, I supposed I had settled on the right clothes.

As we entered the lane of Hunter's mansion, a long queue of cars told me just how big this party was. Tony appeared unimpressed and maneuvered into a spot at the corner, but I had a hard time closing my mouth. "How many guests is he expecting?"

"Can't say. Usually, there are a hundred to a hundred and fifty. If his parents are gone, the number might well get up to three hundred."

Heck, I didn't even know that many people if I counted all my friends, family, and their pets together. We walked up the drive then climbed the marble steps to the door with the bowed top. The music blasted through the wood so we figured we didn't need to ring the doorbell. Tony jiggled the handle, and it opened easily.

Sean Paul's *She Doesn't Mind* was blaring from the many speakers as we entered. Bodies bumped and ground against each other in salacious moves I only knew from films. Several boys shouted a conversation over the noise and drank beer from bottles while groping the butts of the girls with them. Some people kissed in the dim light.

I clung to Tony's comforting biceps. "Oh my God, don't leave me alone in this place."

He laughed, or so I thought when his ribcage shook slightly, because I couldn't really hear him. But his arm pressed my hands tighter to his body as he pulled me into the mass of people. Not all of them were kids. It seemed Hunter had a lot of older friends, too, ranging from sixteen to about twenty-five.

A small group of girls from my history class gathered in the middle of the room. Simone Simpkins grabbed my arm when we passed them. I had to lip-read to understand that she wanted me to join them.

"I'll get you something to drink," Tony shouted in my ear.

I nodded and watched him walk away with a weird quiver in my stomach. What if he never found his way back to me in this blasted place? The distance he put between us was quickly filled with the throng of strangers. Shit, I shouldn't have let him go.

Turning back to the girls, I tried to join in the conversation, but mostly I just stood there and nodded, pretending to understand what they said. Simone handed me a bottle of Bud Ice when Tony hadn't come back after ten minutes. Parched by the heat in the room, anything cool was welcome. I wet my lips with the beer then licked it off. Okay, this stuff wasn't half bad. I took a real sip. A little bitter, but quite palatable. I had downed half of the bottle when my head started to feel dizzy.

Across the room I thought I spotted Tony. I waved goodbye to the girls and headed off toward the back. The crowd thinned a little there, and I could actually move without rubbing against other people's sweat. But Tony was nowhere in sight.

A high arch in the wall connected this room to the kitchen. I headed there and found Ryan standing in the doorway, leaning one shoulder against the wall. The sleeves of his black shirt were rolled up to his elbows, and the jeans he wore were ripped at the hems. Black was a color I loathed on Tony. It made him look way too demonic. With Ryan it was different. The top buttons undone, he looked mysterious. Kind of sexy. Him looking like the devil was cool.

His gaze flickered my way then stayed as he sipped his beer, watching as I drew closer.

It would have been plain impolite not to say hello to the host, so I stopped before him and lifted my hand in greeting. The music wasn't as loud back here, and I actually caught his *hi*.

"You have a nice place. So full of…people," I said, feeling awkward and a little stupid for not knowing how to start a cool conversation.

"Yeah, thanks." He moved away from the wall and leaned closer to me so I could hear him. "It was about time Mitchell brought you here. He kept you away from this place long enough."

Huh? I frowned. *Tony* was the reason I hadn't been invited to any of Ryan's parties yet? That bloody wretch. But then he probably figured I wouldn't feel comfortable among this drinking lot and with all the noise. I, the idiot that I am, proved his point the second we came here by clinging to his arm like a frightened cat.

"Do you know where he is?" I said into Ryan's ear, thankful that I didn't need to shout and damage my vocal cords even more.

"Nope." He took another swig from his beer.

Sighing, I sipped mine too, not liking it very much anymore. I grimaced. Ryan suddenly took me by the wrist and pulled me into the kitchen. He placed his beer down on a counter, popped open a can of soda, then lifted the beer bottle out of my palm and replaced it with the Sprite, closing my fingers around it.

"You shouldn't drink beer," he said in a stern tone. "Especially not in this place."

Yeah, I didn't want to end up someone's groping puppet, like most of the other drunken girls. Thankful for the Sprite, I washed away the bitter aftertaste of the Bud Ice in my mouth.

"You did really well today." A smile slipped to his lips.

"I was lousy. And you know it. I still don't get why you chose me to play on your team."

Shrugging, he drank from my discarded bottle. "I don't know. Maybe I just want you there."

Jeez, the teasing in his voice made the hair on my arms stand on end.

"Do a little endurance training every day, and you'll be a capable player."

I'd always screwed up at athletics. I even tried jogging a few mornings at the beginning of this summer to get in better shape, but it didn't work for me. Half a mile was the most I could manage before trudging back home, panting and frustrated. "I guess I'm lacking the motivation to do that. I'm like a lame duck at running."

"What you need is a personal trainer."

That made me laugh. "You want the job?"

Ryan pursed his lips and studied me for a moment as though I had just offered him good money for stinking work. He shrugged. "Sure, why not? If you promise to show some enthusiasm, I promise to be there."

That sounded like an interesting offer. After all, I had to work on my endurance if I wanted to last an entire soccer game. I certainly didn't want to give Blondie any more ammunition to use against me, especially if I broke down after the first half. Her satisfaction would ruin me. And Tony needed to see I was fit for more than just playing stupid video games with him.

Yeah. Training, it is.

Strangely enough, the thought of having Hunter coaching me sent a shiver of anticipation through me. He was the captain of the soccer team. It felt like an honor to personally train with him, and it sure would lift my status at school from average to super cool.

"Okay, deal."

He gave a slow nod. "We'll start Monday morning."

Great. That meant suicide was delayed one more day. His gaze locking with mine promised I wouldn't entirely regret my decision.

Someone shouted his name behind me. "We're starting a game of pool. Are you in?"

Ryan pushed away from the counter. "There in a sec." Then he ran the cool mouth of his beer bottle along my cheek. "Enjoy the night. And whatever you do, stay away from the strawberries."

Dumbstruck, I stood rooted to the spot as he brushed past me and walked away, chuckling.

I swallowed a huge swig of Sprite to cool down. Susan Miller came in at that moment. Her face lit up when her gaze fell on me. She rushed over. "Hey, look who it is! Now we're both on the team. And honestly—" She paused, and her eyes darted left then right to make sure we were alone in the room. Her voice dropped a notch, too. "I've never seen a prettier house than this. I've wanted to come to Hunter's parties for ages, but he never noticed me in school. I don't think he even knew my name until I told him at tryouts."

"Yeah, me too." Or so I'd thought until yesterday when I found out he actually knew my name.

"Will you wear your sports clothes for training or get a real soccer jersey?" Susan seemed so excited, I couldn't understand her enthusiasm. What girl would voluntarily play soccer? Well, if there wasn't a guy on the team she wanted to recognize her anyway.

I shrugged. "No idea. Think I'll start with what I have. Just shorts and a tee. Anything else is too expensive to buy with my allowance." And no way would I wear those horrible shoes with spikes on their soles. But the outfit was nothing that really concerned me. "Listen, did you see Tony anywhere this evening?"

"Not after you came in with him earlier. Why?"

"Haven't seen him much. I just wonder where he is." I threw my empty soda can in the trash and pulled an apologetic face. "Mind if I go looking for him?"

Susan was cool. "Do that. I'll find you later."

I went back into the hall and wandered around the ground floor, hoping to find Tony somewhere. But the shoving and bumping of sweat-drenched people soon got on my nerves, and I kept closer to the walls instead. When I reached an arch leading to another room, I peeked inside. No blond caught my eye. My shoulders slumped with disappointment. But then a few guys shifted to the side, and I spotted a pool table and someone leaning over it in an eye-catching way.

By now I was pretty good at recognizing Hunter's

black hair.

He held the cue low over the green felt, aiming the tip at the white ball. Some colored balls fanned out on the table too, but as it looked he was going for the black eight.

"Come on, Ryan, give a friend a chance. You can't hole the ball just yet."

I pivoted to the left to see who was pleading with Hunter. I didn't know the tall boy's name, but the look on his face was hilarious. One would think his life depended on Ryan's hit or miss.

"What's your problem, Justin?" Still working on positioning the cue perfectly, Hunter grinned. "Afraid, your mama's going to find out you're playing for money?"

Just then I noticed the stack of dollar bills at the edge of the table. They seemed to have a sum of about one hundred bucks in the pot. My jaw dropped. Fifty from each? I didn't get half as much pocket money in one month.

"My mama doesn't give a damn. But I *really, really need* this Spiderman comic. It's an original," Justin whined.

I felt really bad for him. Intrigued how the game would end, I moved around the edge of the wall and stood facing Hunter across the room. Narrowed eyes and knitted brows gave away how tense he was. The cue moved backward just a couple of inches. He'd shoot any moment.

But then his dark eyes looked up…and remained fixed on me. His body froze, only his chest moved with each breath. Heads turned in my direction. My heart drummed a little faster, and with all the attention, my cheeks warmed uncomfortably.

I grimaced. "Is something wrong?"

Ryan didn't answer, but Justin victory-punched the air as he rushed to my side. He laid his arm around my shoulders, grinning like a loon. "You just saved my life, hun."

"Ah…*yes*." My gaze switched back to Hunter. "And how so?"

He started grinning, too, but didn't seem as happy as the guy next to me. More like he knew crap was about to fall.

"He can't play when someone's watching him," Justin almost sang into my ear. "Totally screws up then."

"But you *all* are watching him," I pointed out.

At the back of the room, someone laughed. "Yeah, but we're not girls."

Chuckling, Hunter straightened and chalked the tip of his cue, lips tight, eyes set on me. Although my being there obviously amused him, I didn't want to trouble him, especially where money had a hand in the pie.

"Sorry," I croaked. "I'll leave you guys alone then."

"Uh-uh, no way, hun!" Justin's arm remained firm around my shoulders. "You're my insurance to get that comic book. You stay."

His antics made me laugh, even though I felt like a traitor.

Ryan, who hadn't said one word in all that time, slid his tongue over his bottom lip, then the left corner of his mouth tilted up. He took a deep breath and leaned over the table once more. Everyone kept silent. Justin crossed his fingers next to my face, no doubt praying for Hunter's miss.

I never thought a single shot could get an entire room this tense. Including me. Ryan cleared his throat, his gaze moving back and forth between me and the white ball. Suddenly he dropped his forehead to the edge of the table and laughed. "Take your money, Andrews. I give up."

The room cheered as though the unthinkable had

just happened. Justin pressed a kiss to my cheek and hurried to grab the bills. I stood rooted to the spot, staring at Ryan, who now braced his palms on the pool table and hung his head. But when he looked up, there was a flash of amusement in his eyes again.

"I'm so sorry," I mouthed, not even trying to raise my voice over the other guys' celebration.

"*You* are banned from this room," he mouthed back, a smirk on his lips. Then he walked around the table, slowly, measuring me with each step he took. I pressed a little harder against the wall, welcoming the coolness seeping through my top.

He stopped right in front of me, the cue in one hand, the other placed against the wall next to my head. "You just cost me fifty bucks," he drawled with a smile.

"Yeah, I know." I put on a sad puppy look. "But he *really, really needs* this comic book."

That made him laugh. "Siding with the enemy. I should have known." With his hand on my back, he ushered me through the arch in the wall, back into the main hall. "For tonight, this room is off limits for you."

"Oh why?" Playfully pouting, I glanced up at his roguish eyes. "It's so much fun to watch you...screw up."

He didn't let his smile slip as he leaned in a little closer. "Off you go."

Chapter 4

I wiggled my fingers at Hunter and left the guys to their game. It was time to look for Tony, anyway. But finding him in a place brimming with two hundred people was impossible. On the plus side, I ran into a few more friends of mine, and Megon Johnson introduced me to her older brother and a few of his companions. One offered to get me another drink. When he suggested Bud Ice, I told him I didn't drink alcohol.

"Fruit juice then?"

"Sounds good."

He got me berry soda in a glass and popped in a straw. Wearing a hat, he looked a little like Bruno Mars. He made an interesting conversation partner over the next hour during which he refilled my soda three times. Eventually, I could see his lips moving but wasn't really getting what he was saying. I also felt the need to frown a lot and lean against the wall for support in the suddenly swaying room.

"You okay?" the guy asked.

The guy with the hat. Did he tell me his name? And when did his twin brother come in? The twin melted into him, then appeared again. Something was very off here. I rubbed my brow. "Not so sure," I said, having trouble getting the words out. I also spoke extra slowly in case he was having the same trouble as me and wouldn't understand a thing.

The world tipped, and suddenly I was in his arms.

"Whoa, girl, you meant it when you said you didn't drink, huh?"

I smiled at his face so close to mine. Sure I meant it. What did he think? That I was a liar? I picked up his hat and planted it on my head. "My turn to be Bruno for a while."

"Hey, what's going on here?"

"Tony?" I rejoiced, trying to locate where his

voice had come from. And then he was right behind me, pulling me away from Mr. Mars without his hat. I turned in Tony's arms and beamed at his oh-so-worried face. "Where have you been all night? I tried so hard to find you."

"Where did you look? At the bottom of the punch?"

I decided I didn't have to understand that and let him pull me to the rear of the house, into the kitchen. "Whoop," I slurred with a loopy smile as he grabbed my waist and lifted me onto the counter. He usually stood half a head taller than me, but sitting here, we were eye to eye, which I really liked. He had such pretty blue eyes.

His hands planted firmly beside my hips, he stood in between my dangling legs. This awkward pose made my brain go wishy-washy and majorly turned me on. I dipped forward and touched my forehead to his, grinning as I stared into those sapphire gems.

Tony laughed, but it sounded nothing like his normal, easy laugh. He straightened me on the counter. "How many drinks did you have?"

"Hey, why so worried?"

"How *many*, Lisa?"

Not liking his commanding tone, I sighed

heavily, puffing my bangs out of my view. "There was this half bottle of beer, and then some Sprite. The soda. One—or four—glasses…I think."

"Soda?"

"Berry soda."

"Shit." He laughed again. It sounded nervous. "Your mom's going to strangle me if I take you home drunk like this."

"I'm not drunk," I protested. "You know I don't drink alco-*hole*."

When a certain bimbo bounced into the kitchen like a doe in a marigold meadow, I thought I was going to puke. She totally ignored me and flashed Tony a flirtatious smile that set my stomach to nausea. "Anthony, you promised to dance with me."

"*Anthony, you promised to dance with me,*" I iterated like a three-year-old.

That drew her attention to me. "What's wrong with *her?*"

"She just had a little too much of the punch. I'll be with you in a minute."

He was going to dance with Chloe? *No!* I wanted to tell him he couldn't, but a sudden lethargy settled over me and made me dip my head to his shoulder. "I'm so tired. Can we go home?"

"Aw, come on, Anthony. You're not going to leave already. It's only eleven." Jeez, how I hated Barbie's voice. "Take her upstairs to one of Hunter's guest rooms. She can sleep there."

"And not bother you any longer?" I managed to moan, tilting my head in her direction, but unable to open my eyes. Her annoyed snort didn't bother me.

"You don't want to do that." Another person seemed to have joined our conversation. Hunter. But what was he talking about?

"In her state, she's not safe in any of the guest rooms. You know how the parties go on the later it gets. Take her to my room."

"What?" Tony and I shouted simultaneously. I was sitting straight with my eyes wide open. The thought of sleeping in Ryan Hunter's room shocked me something awful. But why Tony was agitated I couldn't figure out.

Ryan rolled his eyes. *Mmm, sexy.* He could do that quite well.

"Don't be ridiculous, guys. She'll be awake and gone before I even get upstairs."

There was a tense pause.

"Hell, do it already, Anthony, and come back fast." *Barbie.*

Tony pressed his lips together.

What was he supposed to do again? The answer escaped me.

"Come on, Liz." He pulled me off the counter and walked me to the door. But a sudden lack of control over my feet made me stumble sideways, knocking into something cold and shiny.

"Pardon me," I said to the fridge.

Ryan caught me before I knocked into more kitchen appliances. "Didn't I tell you to stay away from the strawberries?" he growled into my ear.

"Strawberries? There was one in my last soda." I grinned. "It was yummy."

"Yummy, all right." He chuckled as he swept me up in his arms. "I'll carry her to my room, Mitchell. You can grab her when you go. Or come back for her in the morning."

"You sure?" There it was again, Tony's worried voice.

"Yes. Go dance with Chloe or she'll pester me next."

The music grew fainter as Ryan climbed the stairs with me. I flung my arms around his neck and leaned my head on his shoulder. "You don't like dancing with Chloe?" I murmured.

He chuckled. "Would you?"

"I don't like her, period."

"And I know exactly why that is."

"Really?" I breathed deep, inhaling his aftershave mingling with the scent of his heated skin. "You smell good."

For some reason, that made him laugh. "Time to go to bed, Matthews."

He shoved open a door and carried me backward over the threshold. Next I was placed on a soft mattress. The pillow bore the same musky scent that clung to Ryan. I drew in a long breath.

He slipped off my shoes and pulled a blanket over my bare legs. "You comfortable?"

"I'm not sure. But can you check if my head has sprouted helicopter blades?"

With my eyes closed, I felt his hand raking through my hair. "That will go away when you sleep. If you need anything, the light switch is right in front of your nose and the bathroom is the next door on the left." He paused. "Did you hear me?"

"Light, nose. Toilet, left. Gotcha." I gave him a thumbs-up, sleep already tugging at me. "Hunter?"

"Hm?"

"Sorry about the pool game."

He chuckled. "Sleep tight, princess."

Something brushed over my cheek. Very gently. Fingers? I couldn't tell as I drifted off to careening dreams.

*

A door banged shut. Jolting upright, I found myself in the center of a bed in a moonlit room I didn't recognize. The figure standing in front of me seemed slightly familiar, though.

"Hunter?"

"You're still here?" Ryan moaned. My presence didn't stop him from unbuttoning his shirt and tossing it in a corner of the room along with his sneakers.

My brain roared like mad. I rubbed my brow. "Where is *here* exactly? And why are you undressing?"

The moonlight cast a silvery look to his features as he studied me. "Well, for one, this is my room. And second, that thing you're lying on is my bed. Since I don't usually sleep in clothes, I figured I'd just take them off." He spoke slowly and in a slightly slurred way. I rubbed my temples, having trouble following this conversation.

The blurry events of the previous evening crept up in my memory. "Is the party over?"

"Someone puked on the floor. Yeah. Party's over." His deep breath was audible in the silent room. "I swear, next time Claudia brings her strawberry soda, I'm going to kick a girl's butt for the first time in my life. Harmless, my ass."

I glanced at my wristwatch. The clock face should've been glowing in the dark, but as soon as I tried to focus, dizziness made me groan. "What time is it?"

"Three."

"A.m.?" I cried.

"It's dark outside. Of course it's a.m."

Slamming back the covers, I jumped out of bed. But gravity was a bitch, and I stumbled to the floor. I patted around for my shoes. I should have been home hours ago. My mom was going to kill me.

I tried to stand again. "Where are my shoes?"

"What are you doing?"

Panicking! Because I felt trapped in a strange house. "Going home!"

God, the pain in my head snarled at me to take it easy. And speaking fast was impossible.

"Whoa." Ryan pushed down on my shoulders

until I sat on the bed again. "So not a good idea. Since we already agreed that it's the dead of night…and you're sixteen…and drunk—"

"Drunk? *No.*" I never drank alcohol. And soda sure wouldn't make my brain so spongy. But I had to admit something was seriously wrong with either me or the room, since everything was spinning in a very uncomfortable way.

Hunter waved a dismissive hand at me. "Whatever. I can't let you do that."

"Do what?"

"Walk alone."

I frowned. "You want to come with me?" Strange. Shouldn't Tony be around to drive me home?

"It's a mile and a half to your house. That's three for me to walk. I'm positive I won't make that tonight." The mattress sank under his weight as he lowered next to me. "So if you really want to go home, I'll have to drive you. But right now, I'd rather not."

Even sitting, Hunter swayed in front of me. But since the room was doing that too, I wasn't sure if he really was or if I was having some kind of weird hallucinations. "So what do I do now?"

"I'd say lay back. Sleep. And worry about

everything tomorrow."

"What about you?"

He looked around the room, rubbing his neck. "The floor is hard. And I'm beat. There's room for two in that bed." He made his last statement sound like a question.

I was getting sick—and not because of his request to sleep in the same bed as me. My stomach rolled. I felt the sour taste of soda traveling up my gullet. There was only one way to avoid puking all over this strange bed and floor. I had to get horizontal.

Dropping to my side, I buried my cheek in the pillow. I groaned, keeping one eye open, and focused on the top of the lamp on the nightstand. If only I could grab my brain and stop it from spinning.

"Good choice, Matthews," Ryan rumbled and lay down beside me. He probably took my silence as an invitation.

Should I care? I wasn't sure.

His head tilted to my side, he grinned—dangerously. "I swear you're safe with me for the next three to six hours. I can't make promises for any time after that, though."

Chapter 5

The sun breaking through the windows woke me the next morning. I felt as if I was drifting out to a restless sea on an unsound airbed. It took a few seconds for the eerie swaying to stop so that I could focus.

My cheek rested on a pillow smelling of pine trees and warmth. I inhaled deeply, wanting to keep that scent, and opened my eyes to stare at the sensual lips of Ryan Hunter. My hand on his naked chest rose and fell with his slow, even breaths.

Holy cow, what the hell happened? I was in bed with the captain of the soccer team. Heck, I should have never gone to that party.

Now, my only thought was *run*. But shock kept me pinned to the bed as I became aware of the entangled position Ryan and I had taken on in our sleep. Lying on my right, my left leg was slung over his hip. My calf rested neatly on his groin. He lay on his back, his left leg bent so that I wouldn't be able to withdraw mine. I tried to stop my body from shivering. No chance.

Not daring to wake him, I didn't move, frantically running through the options I had. Great, there were none. I was trapped.

Maybe if I lay still, pretending to be fast asleep, until he woke up and got out of bed first, then I could sneak out after him and be gone before he noticed. I would have slapped myself for that idea if I could've removed my hand from his warm chest.

And a firm chest it was. He must lift weights besides playing soccer. As if my eyes had their own mind, they traveled down his gorgeous body. A thin trail of dark hair led south from his navel over his flat stomach until it vanished under the waistband of his jeans. His bent leg seemed amazingly long. I'd never paid attention, but he must've been more than a head taller than me.

My gaze swept up to his neck and the part of his face not covered with his arm. A lean jaw and a perfect, straight nose. He sported an overnight shadow that begged to be rubbed. I resisted. Under his left ear was an old scar, about an inch long. One would never notice unless close to him, like I was now.

Suddenly his lips twitched.

"I can feel you staring at me," he said in the softest wake-up voice I'd ever heard. "I only hope you're a girl and not one of the drunken guys."

My breath caught in my chest. I jerked my hand back from him. Not taking his arm away from his face yet, he reached down with his other hand and slowly ran his palm over my naked thigh in the direction of my butt.

"Yep, definitely female," he purred.

In panic, I held his hand in place. "Move another inch, Hunter, and you're a dead man."

"Matthews?" Surprised amusement filled his chuckle. Unlike me, he seemed relaxed enough.

A strange heat rose from my gut to my head as I studied his hand on my bare skin. Wearing nothing but jeans and a black wristwatch, he looked more like a guy from the many posters on the walls of Simone Simpkins' bedroom than the boy I knew from school.

I felt awkward for not letting go of his hand on my leg, but I was too scared he'd continue the path he'd started if I did.

"Tell me, Matthews," he said as he dropped his arm to the pillow and tilted his head to study me with warm eyes. "Why are you in my bed…if I'm not allowed to touch you?"

"I didn't know there were strawberries in the soda," I whined.

His brow furrowed, his lips pursed. "Come again?"

Jeez, did he not realize that he was still holding my leg, and how very uncomfortable—and excited— it made me? "Someone was getting me berry soda all evening." My voice shook slightly. "I didn't realize it was the punch you meant when you said—"

"—not to touch the strawberries," he finished for me, closing his eyes. "Damn, I told her not to punch it too much."

What? The punch? I was pretty sure I'd had a tad too much of that stuff.

A frown creased Ryan's brows as he looked at me again. "Sorry, I don't remember much of the night after I carried you up here. Am I in trouble?"

Considering I still had my clothes on, nothing

had happened during the night. "As far as I remember you were pretty drunk yourself. So I was quite safe from you."

A smirk played around one corner of his mouth. "I'm afraid my time of numb indifference is over." His thumb had started drawing small circles on my skin. "So, unless you're up for some trouble *now*, would you mind moving your leg?"

My eyes widened at his seductive threat.

"What? You know you're not the ugliest girl in the world."

Wow, what a compliment. Idiot. I needed to get out of there. Back to…back to… Damn, Ryan did have a nice smile.

I shoved that thought away and let go of his hand, then pushed his leg down so I could remove mine from his groin. I was out of his bed faster than a bullet. But the aftermath of drinking hit me harder than I expected. The floor rushed to me or I rushed to it, I couldn't tell which.

His hands cupped my elbows, and he steadied me before I fell. He waited until my gaze locked with his. "Feel better?"

"Not really." I tried to find my shoes. They lay at the end of the bed, and I wiggled out of his hold to put them on.

Ryan ignored his sneakers and shirt, which lay tossed on the floor. Barefoot, he padded from the room. I followed him down the stairs, gazing at his back. What was it with naked skin all of a sudden that made me forget the world around me?

"Hey, Hunter," someone called from the hall to which we descended.

"Morning, Chris," Hunter replied to the boy lying sprawled on the sofa. He walked on as if it was the most natural thing for him to come down from his room with a random girl after a night of partying.

It might be the usual for him, but it sure as hell wasn't for me. I felt my face turn a deep red as heat shot to my cheeks. God, I should have jumped out of his window instead of being subjected to this embarrassment. I hated giving anyone the wrong idea. And there were quite a few leftover guests from last night.

The front door called to me, promising freedom. But Hunter had different ideas and pulled me into the kitchen. When he released my hand, I stood rigid in the middle of the marble floor while he headed for the fridge. He grabbed two bottles of water, unscrewed them, and dropped into each of them a tablet he'd fetched from a cupboard. The tablets were still dissolving as he handed one bottle to me and then leaned against the counter, legs crossed at the ankles, drinking from the other.

I didn't dare take a sip.

"Why so skeptical, Matthews? It will help your headache."

After that innocent-looking berry drink that had landed me in this situation…yeah, I was skeptical. But since he was drinking the same stuff, I figured I was safe. Reluctantly, I sniffed the water then sipped.

"You don't trust me?" He chuckled and drank some more.

"How could I? I woke up with a hangover from soda and with an equally drunk person sleeping next to me half of the night."

"Yeah, sorry about that." He gave me a sheepish grin. "I don't usually get drunk at my own parties. And believe me I'm going to give Claudia an earful for messing with the punch."

I was really starting to loathe that word. And the drink even more so.

"Look, as long as you keep hydrated today, you'll be fine."

I winced, not believing him one second. "It feels

like someone installed a construction site in my head."

"Oh yeah, I know the feeling. If you give me a minute to shower, I'll drive you home."

"No!" Ah hell, panicky shouting wasn't a good idea. I grimaced, pressing my temples until the throbbing eased. "No thanks," I tried again in a calmer tone, just wanting out of this house. "I'll be happy to take the walk and sober up before seeing my parents. My mom will freak out."

"Suit yourself." He walked me to the front door. "Want my sunglasses?"

"Why would I want your sunglasses?" The moment I pulled open the door I knew why. Like a vampire, I flinched back into the shade. And right into his firm chest. Which was still naked. And damn enticing.

He reached around me, holding out his shades which he'd fetched from somewhere. The scent of pure Hunter enveloped me. For a millisecond, the screaming in my aching head stopped, and I was about to faint for a different reason.

"I know what you want." I could hear the mocking smile in his voice when he said it into my ear. I swallowed hard, only then realizing he meant his sunglasses.

Putting on the shades, I pushed away from him and trudged outside, down the steps.

"Matthews," Ryan called after me, and I turned. "We'll start your training tomorrow morning. Be up and ready at five. I'll pick you up."

My jaw hit my chest as he shut the door.

Chapter 6

By half past ten, I slipped through the door of our house. Mom stood in the threshold of the kitchen, with her cell phone in her hand. She looked up, and a relieved smile curved her lips. "Hi, sweetie. Why didn't you take your phone with you? I was just about to call Tony to check if everything was okay."

Praise the Lord for the many nights I'd crashed at Tony's in the past ten years. Mom was so used to it, she didn't expect anything bad when I didn't come home after being out with him. I resisted the urge to cross myself and forced a smile.

"How was the party?" she asked in her innocent, motherly way.

"Good."

"When was it over?"

"Little after three?"

Great, sound anymore guilty, and she'll tie you to the kitchen chair and start a nasty inquisition. Luckily, her frown eased after a second, and she asked me if I wanted anything to eat. Ham and eggs, my favorite breakfast.

The churning of my stomach rebelled like the worst traitor through the room. Please, no food. I couldn't help but gag and wrinkle my face. "No thanks, Mom."

"What is it? Don't you feel well?" She was in front of me before I could escape to the stairs.

I pulled off Hunter's shades and pinched the spot between my eyes. "Nah, all's fine."

"What's with your eyes, honey?"

Shit. I quickly lowered my eyelids and stared at the floor.

Too late. She gasped. "They're totally red. Lisa Isadora Matthews—"

Oh great, the full name. This was going downward.

"Have you been drinking alcohol?"

In contrast to her roar, my voice dropped to a mumble. "Only a little bit. And I didn't know there was alcohol in the soda, I swear."

From there she pulled off the full parental orchestra of scolding. She shouted, she grunted, she called me irresponsible. But the worst thing was, she grounded me.

The only time I would see daylight was soccer training Tuesday and Thursday, and she only gave in to that because I begged on my knees. After all, I couldn't *not* show up for the first week of training when it had been so hard to get onto the team.

Then she brought me a glass of water, hugged me, and said she was happy I didn't get hurt. Duh, she didn't know about my hammering head yet.

Back in my room, I slumped on my bed and made plans for a week trapped inside. At least my to-be-read stack would shrink drastically this way.

Later that day, my phone vibrated on the nightstand, with Tony's name flashing on the display. I pushed the button to cut him off. Just letting it ring wouldn't have been enough. He needed to know that I didn't want to talk to him.

A few moments later, I got a text message.

Tony

Are you mad at me?

Jerk. I wouldn't answer that.

It didn't take long for him to send the next text.

Tony

So it's not a question of *if* but of *how much.*

I clamped my teeth, scowling sinisterly at the phone since he wasn't here to receive the evil glare himself, as I typed:

Me

I woke up in a strange house, in a stranger's bed, with a stranger sleeping next to me. What do you think??

Then I then picked up my book, and read three more lines before my cell beeped again.

Tony

What did Hunter do to you? I'm going to kill him!

He did nothing. He was a perfect gentleman. Unlike you, idiot!

No text came after that. But soon my phone rang again. This time I picked up. "What?"

"I'm sorry."

"I don't care. You forgot me at the party."

He sighed before he replied. "I didn't forget you. It was the middle of the night, and I figured the way you were—"

"Drunk?"

"Yes. I thought it wasn't a good idea to take you home. And risk your mom finding out. You seemed in a good place in Hunter's room. He promised you'd be awake already when he would go to sleep."

"What time did you leave?"

"One. Why?"

Okay, so he couldn't know what happened. "Someone threw up in the hall. The party was over at three."

"Shit." He paused. "So will you come and hang out on the beach with a few of us?"

"I can't. I'm grounded all week. Will Chloe be with you all?"

"Um…yes."

Terrific! Tears of frustration welled up in my eyes.

"You only met her yesterday. I don't see how you can hate her so much."

"You know what I think about bimbos."

"Look, she's not a bimbo," he tried in what should've been a soothing tone. "And I think you two will get along well once you know each other better."

"No thanks. I'd rather stay grounded for the rest of the summer."

"Agh, Liz. Just when did you become so complicated?"

Me—complicated? "Know what? I wish you a nice day at the beach. Now, if you don't mind, I have a book to read." I didn't wait for him to say bye, or anything for that matter, but pushed the disconnect button and tossed the cell into the laundry basket across the room. Screw him and the Barbie clone. Screw them all.

As the first tears came out, I wanted to rip my room apart with the anger I felt. But I was going to spend a lot more time than usual in here in the coming week and I didn't want to live in a mess. So I took it out on my diary. In the evening I watched some TV then went to bed early.

It was still dark when someone shouting my name in a subdued voice woke me. Since there were not many people who called me Matthews, I jerked upright in my bed, my heart banging in my throat. I rushed to the window and found Hunter standing in our yard, dressed in shorts and a black tee.

"Hi," he said and smiled when he saw me. "You don't look like you're ready to go."

I fought to find my voice but kept it low, leaning far out of the window. "How did you know this was my window?"

"I didn't. It was trial and error."

Oh God. "How many windows have you tried?"

"Yours."

Okay. *Okay.* I needed to calm down. The captain of the soccer team was waiting below my window, and I was standing there in my tank top and boy shorts. Duh, it was five in the morning.

"Are you coming?"

"I can't. I'm grounded."

A sly smile played on his lips. "For sleeping with me?"

"For not sleeping in my own bed," I whispered back, fighting to bite down the grin he teased from me.

"How long are you grounded?"

"Until Sunday. But I can come to the practices."

"At least there's that." He scratched his chin, looking around my garden, especially scanning the shed and tree next to my window. "What time do you usually get up in the morning?"

What kind of question was that? "I don't know. Eight, nine, sometimes later."

"So we have at least three hours until someone will expect you downstairs." The left corner of his mouth tilted up, and he flicked his head, motioning for me to move. "Come out."

"What?"

"Get dressed and climb to the roof of the shed. I'll help you down."

A hesitant laugh broke from my throat. "You're crazy."

"*You* are a coward."

"I'm not!"

"Prove it."

That cut me silent.

Tony had used the tree and shed to get into my room since we were nine years old. But with a key to the front door, I had never felt the need to do the same.

"So?" Ryan prompted me.

"Fine. Give me a minute." He was insane, and I was even crazier to agree to his stupid idea. But heck, what did I have to lose? Apart from another week of freedom for a reckless escape from my room.

I traded my jammies for shorts, a white tank top, and sneakers, then wound my hair back into a high ponytail. Hunter was leaning against the trunk of the maple tree when I returned to the window. He straightened when he saw me.

A little shaky at first, I hoisted one leg over the windowsill and then clutched the frame as I let myself down to the roof of the shed.

"Good." Ryan's low voice already sounded nearer than before. "Now hang onto that branch, and I'll get you down."

Huh? "I'll break my neck if I fall." *Goddammit, I should have stayed in my room.*

"I won't let you fall. Promise." He lifted his arms toward me as if intending to catch me.

Breathing deep, I grabbed the nearest branch then stepped off the wood-board roof, suppressing a frightened moan. My feet dangled in front of his face. He stepped closer and ran his hands up my thighs until he had a good grip right beneath my bottom. I swallowed hard and wondered if he had the slightest idea how that made me feel…

"I have you. Let go."

"What?" I cried out, digging my fingers harder into the wood.

He laughed, and I found I quite liked that sound. It felt soothing, somehow. "Let go of the branch, Matthews. *Now.*"

"*Ungh.*" It took all my courage to uncurl my fingers and let him support my weight. As soon as I let go, I clutched his shoulders, and he eased the grip of my legs to wrap his arms around me and let me slide down against his body. When my feet touched firm ground, I looked up at his face.

He didn't immediately release me but let a smile tug on his lips. "Hi."

Chapter 7

The beguiling scent of Hunter enveloped me, just like his arms. Tony had hugged me on countless occasions. But this was different. It screamed in comparison to the placid emotions I experienced when my best friend hugged me. This was mind-blastingly, blood-boilingly exciting. A thrill went through me. I stepped out of his embrace.

"Can we go?" he asked, making no effort to hide his amusement at my obvious discomfort.

"Where to?"

"The beach."

That was about two miles away. Was he kidding? I'd probably drop dead halfway. But I wasn't a whiner—I hoped. I nodded, and we started off at a slow pace for which I was grateful. In the morning, the street was unnaturally silent. I couldn't remember when I had last been out at this time of day. Five was way too early to do sports. Seriously. The normally bright facades of the houses lining our street all appeared in a monotone bluish-gray now.

"So your parents got angry because you didn't get home Saturday night?" he said with perfectly even breathing after the first quarter mile.

Did he really expect me to jog *and* talk? My breathing was erratic, but I managed to say, "No. My parents thought I crashed at Tony's. Which is fine with them."

"You do that often?"

"You sound like you disapprove."

He only cut me a sharp sideways glance. Heck, what was that? Did he really care?

"So why the grounding?" he asked as we passed a crossroads and neared the ocean. The sound of waves crashing on the beach drifted to us, breaking the silence of the morning.

"My mom saw my red eyes and figured I'd been

drinking. Crap—" I panted. Sweat trailed down my neck, my back, and between my breasts. "I forgot your sunglasses."

"No worries. You can give them to me tomorrow before practice."

How did he do this? Run so far and still speak to me like he was lounging on the sofa. Gasping for air, I only nodded. The beach came into sight, and relief filled me. A few more steps, I told myself and pushed harder. Then my feet hit sand.

And I collapsed.

Dropping to the beach like a sack of flour, I rolled onto my back and gazed at the soft pink sky.

Ryan stood over me. "What are you doing?"

"Dying."

"No, you're not. Get up, we're not done."

"*I* am." My breaths sounded like those of a rasping woman on her deathbed. "But don't mind me. You just go on. I'm sure in a few hours someone will come and scrape me off the pavement…dig me out of the sand…whatever."

Amazing how the sound of his laughter made me wish for the strength to stand up and continue running just to be near him again. Luck was on my side today. A moment later, he lowered to the sand, too.

Hunkered by my feet, he…untied my shoe?

"Hey, what the heck—!" I pulled my leg away. "You don't steal from a dying person."

He lifted his palms in defense. "Fine, then take them off yourself."

"What? Why?" Shocked and a little curious, I propped on my elbows and watched as he untied his laces. Hope filled me. "We're going to take a swim now to cool off after all that training?"

"Nope. The little run was only warm-up. The training begins here."

"You can't be serious." What was it with him and warming up all the time? I was heated enough when we left my street.

His eyebrow arched up. "What are you willing to bet on it?"

Shit. He *was* serious. Ready to slump back and bawl, I clamped my teeth instead and gathered what little dignity I had left then sat up. I slipped out of my sneakers and hid them with Ryan's close to the rocks and out of temptation from passersby.

If I thought running to the beach was exhausting, then I sure didn't know what it was like to jog barefoot in the sand. The muscles in my calves took on a burn that became unbearable after only a couple hundred feet.

I shot him a look filled with loathing as I struggled to keep pace with him. He smiled, making me gnash my teeth.

"Do your parents know about this sadistic side of yours?"

He playfully tugged at my ponytail. "What can I say? You bring out my best side."

"Ah, great. I feel so special now." Each step became increasingly heavy as if my limbs were weighed down with stones. "How far are we going?"

"I never ran this route before, but I guess it's about a half-mile. You know the houses at Misty Beach?"

I nodded. Everyone knew them. It was a place for the rich and wealthy. "Your parents own a house down there?"

"Yep."

I wasn't surprised. After seeing the palace he lived in last night, it was expected that the Hunters would have another beach house here. But it was funny, after the last two days, Ryan didn't seem at all like the insufferable playboy I thought him to be whenever I passed him in the school corridors. He was quite likable. Nice, even.

Just not right now. I scowled. The fine sand sunk under my feet and it felt like running on pudding. Every exposed square inch of me glistened with sweat; my drenched top clung to my skin.

When Misty Beach came into view, his fingers curled around my upper arm, and he was dragging me. I stumbled along next to him, crying for water. "I swear I'm going to drink up the ocean."

"Chin up, Matthews. We're almost there." So said the king's most trusted torturer.

He led me to the prettiest house at this strip of the beach. Painted in white, it had a wraparound wooden porch with nice rattan furniture and even a porch swing. From the potted plant on the broad railing, he fetched a set of keys and let us inside.

Average sized, the bungalow had a kitchen and maybe two or three bedrooms in the back. We entered into a cozy sitting room, with comfy couches, a flat-screen TV, and an amazingly wide bookshelf. Someone really liked to read out here.

The modern door without a handle fell shut and locked behind us. Ryan left me leaning against the wall and grabbed two bottles of water from the fridge. He tossed one to me.

Ah, liquid heaven. Water had never tasted this good.

My pulse stayed in higher spheres for a little longer, but I found I could talk without gasping for air like a dying fish. "So, great tormentor, why did we run on the beach? Was it just for your personal pleasure of seeing me suffer?"

He rolled his eyes with a half-smile that not even Tony could beat. "Why do you think so badly of me?"

"I don't know. Maybe because I lost my lungs somewhere on the way here? Or because my legs are on fire?" I walked over to the couch and leaned my butt against the backrest, arms folded over my chest.

"Oh, come on now. We jogged over two miles and you're still standing. That's great. And running in the sand will strengthen your legs a lot better than the pavement. Since we only run on grass at soccer, you need to get used to the additional…"

"Torture?" I helped him out when he paused to search for the right word.

"Exactly." He pushed aside my damp bangs with a finger, took my empty bottle, and tossed both with a high arc into the trash can just outside the kitchen door.

I fixed my ponytail then swept my forearm across

my brows. Sweaty as my arm was, it didn't help much.

The sound of footsteps clinking on the porch caught our attention. For a reason that escaped me, we both stiffened.

The shock on Ryan's face as he glanced first at the door then at me prickled my skin into goose bumps. Without warning, he rushed toward me, knocking me over the backrest of the couch. Together we rolled to the floor. Keys rattled in the lock as I landed on him, and a rush of air exploded out of his lungs.

"Who is it?" I hissed, glaring down at his face. In this awkward position, I couldn't help but notice the beautiful color his eyes were. Like the tiger's eye my mother kept in her collection of gemstones.

"Can only be my mom." Using a little pressure to my hip, he steered me closer to the couch as he rolled me off him, then he clapped his hand over my mouth. Duh, as if I was going to scream.

My heart pounded like that of a criminal during a bank robbery as we listened to Mrs. Hunter walk into the room and put something heavy on the floor. Sounded like boxes. She carried one after the other into the kitchen.

"She's stocking the fridge," Ryan murmured with

his mouth to my ear.

Great. Who would pack a fridge at six in the morning? But then she probably wanted it done before she went to work. When she went for the third round, I pulled Ryan's hand off my mouth and said in a fierce whisper, "Why are we hiding here?"

"My parents don't like me bringing random girls to this place. Unless you want to be introduced as my girlfriend, I suggest you stay down."

Okay then. I scowled at him from the half-inch space between us, wondering how, in only twenty-four hours, I could land in such an intimate position with Hunter—twice.

A breath of relief whizzed out of me when his mother finally left the house and the door locked. A minute passed before Ryan pushed to his feet. He held his hand out for me, but I didn't move a limb.

"You sure your dad isn't on his way, too?" Heavy cynicism laced my voice.

"Yes, I'm sure. He never comes here during the week." He grabbed my hand and tugged. "Get up."

I let him help me stand. "Next time you feel the need to knock me over, I'd appreciate a little warning first."

"Sure thing!" He went to the rear of the house

and came back with a towel that he wiped over his face then tossed at me.

"Ew." He didn't really expect me to use the same towel he'd already marked with his sweat? "I don't know how a little running together got us to this level of intimacy." But since he ignored my annoyed look and walked outside, I figured I just had to overcome that part of me and wipe my sweating body with it. Rubbing my neck, I followed Ryan onto the porch and found him lounging on the swing.

Drenched in my sweat, I tossed the towel at his face with deadly aim. But he caught it. "Let's go back," I muttered.

"Are we in a hurry, Matthews?"

I refused to take a seat anywhere on this porch but leaned my shoulder against the post next to the wooden steps that led down to the beach. "Not really. But I won't stay in a place where I have to sign a marriage license to be welcome."

"She won't come back."

"I don't care." Wow, that was a growl. I didn't know I could actually sound this pissed.

"Fair enough." He sighed and rose from the swing. "Let me just get the ball, then we can go."

"The ball?"

But he was already gone and came out a little later with a backpack that had an ominous round swell. He stuffed the towel and another bottle of water into the backpack then strapped it over his shoulders. The keys he dumped back into the potted plant.

Fortunately, he didn't make me run again. We strolled along the beach, and I welcomed the cool rush of water around my ankles.

Safely out of sight of his house, I finally relaxed. "Why did you bring the ball?"

"You need to practice kicking and catching. The beach is perfect for that."

Okay, that didn't sound too bad. But I underestimated Hunter. What he truly meant I found out when we reached the place where we'd hidden our shoes.

Chapter 8

I wiped the sand off my soles and slipped into my sneakers. Ryan took a position about thirty feet away from me. The ball in the sand, his right foot on top of it, he shouted, "I want you to stop the ball."

"Ah, okay. Just—" *Whoosh*, the ball raced at me. I let out a small shriek, but caught the ball to my chest.

He looked at me as if I'd forgotten to put on clothes this morning. "This is soccer. You're not supposed to use your hands."

How was I to know what he wanted from me when he tried to kill me with a soccer ball?

"Kick it back."

I did as he said, dispersing a great deal more sand than he'd done when he kicked it. Ryan shot again. Same speed, same aim. Right at my chest. I caught it.

"No hands, Matthews!"

Okay, this was really getting on my nerves. I sent it flying back to him.

He kicked.

This time I stepped to the side and let the ball zoom past me.

"What was that?" Disbelief marred his face as he came toward me.

"You said no hands. Want me to catch it with my teeth or what?"

He laughed. "I strongly suggest you don't do that. During a game you will have to stop the ball. But you're not allowed to use your hands. So you use your body to block it. Your shoulders, or head, but mostly your chest."

"Aha. There's only one problem with that." I cupped my boobs with both hands. "I've got these!"

Struck silent, his gaze traveled from my eyes downward and didn't return. The spark in his eyes almost scared me. Like I was Snow White and he was the...*Hunter*. In fact, I didn't want to even imagine what thoughts were crossing his mind right then. I snapped my fingers between our faces. "Eyes up here."

He obeyed. Reluctantly. The sliver of an impish smile crept to his lips.

"Enough training for one morning." I could barely keep my voice even. "I want to be back before my mom finds out I'm gone."

He agreed, and I managed to convince him that we only run half the way then walk the rest. I didn't want to break down in front of my house. But when we arrived, I faced the next hurdle. Dad was already gone to work, but Mom was in the kitchen, and there was no way to sneak inside without her noticing.

"I'm so screwed," I whined, hiding behind a tree on the other side of the street.

Ryan cupped my chin with an unexpectedly tender hand and made me look at his face. "Do you always give up that quickly?"

"Apparently, *you* don't," I muttered with clipped annoyance for his lack of understanding of my misery. "So what do you suggest?"

"We get you inside the same way we got you out."

"The window?"

"Exactly." His head slightly angled, he lifted his

brows with encouragement.

"Tony has been climbing in and out of there for years. But I don't see how I can do it."

"Mitchell has been climbing into your room?"

"Yes. But I need a ladder to get onto the roof of the shed. And as far as I know, we don't have a ladder." My shoulders slumped in defeat.

"Why?"

"Why what?"

"Why does he climb through your window?" The question was a snarl, and his brow furrowed.

"Can we please stay focused? I'm grounded and I need to sneak into my own house."

He glared at me. Then, with his jaw tight, he nodded. "All right. Come on." He pulled at my top and hauled me across the street. I could only hope my mom wasn't peeking out the window.

As we rounded the house and I could hide beside the shed, I felt a little safer. Still, there was this problem of getting on top of it.

Ryan scanned the tree. "I believe Mitchell climbs up there to get onto the roof?"

"Um, yes. But you aren't asking me to climb a tree now, are you?"

He gave a light snort. Then he tested the edge of

the shed's roof by jumping and hanging on to it. It was solid. "Come here, Matthews," he ordered as he planted himself in a wide stance with his back to the shed's door.

"What are you doing?"

"Giving you a lift." He laced his fingers in front of his hips. Obviously, I was supposed to step in there.

"No way."

"Don't be a baby. I already proved I can hold you, remember? Twice."

He was right. Still, that didn't take the queasy feeling out of my stomach. If at all, the memory increased my flurry. In the end, with my mom downstairs, I figured I didn't have much of a choice. With a resigned sigh, I stepped toward him and held on to his shoulders while he bent his knees to make it easier for me to place my foot into the hold he provided.

"Ready?" he teased as we were on eye level.

"Not at all," I replied, a little shaky.

"See you tomorrow." Then he shot me up into space. I had no time to think, which might have been a good thing, but just grabbed onto the roof's edge and hoisted myself over with Ryan's help.

From there it was an easy walk to get back into

my room. Once my feet were planted on the solid floor, I turned back toward him. My knees still wobbly from the adventure and the fear of getting caught, I grimaced. "I don't think we should do this again."

"Why not?"

"I'm dead if my parents catch me." And it wasn't really a matter of *if* but *when*.

"They won't."

"What if?"

"Matthews, they won't. Now shut up and go have a shower."

Agh, he really didn't understand my dilemma. I gritted my teeth. "Well, I'm not coming tomorrow. There's training with the team anyway. I won't survive two rounds of torture on the same day."

"Yeah. Right." He laughed. "Wednesday. Five o'. Be dressed this time. And Matthews—don't make me climb up there and fetch you."

Though my body screamed at the torture Ryan had put me through this morning, my mind spun with a strange anticipation. He was going to train with me again. I smiled to myself as I headed for the shower. Damn, I never knew I was that much of a masochist.

The hot spray of water loosened my burning muscles. I could have spent the whole day in there. Ah heck, being grounded, I didn't have much else to do anyway, so I enjoyed an extended treat in the shower. When the water finally turned cold on me, I slipped out, wrapped my body in a soft, white towel, and walked back to my room.

As I opened the door, a shriek escaped me.

"What the hell are you doing here?"

"Waiting on your merciful return from the bathroom." Tony grinned from where he lay on my bed.

I shot a glance over my shoulder, hoping my mom hadn't heard my scream.

"Don't panic. Beth already knows I'm here."

"What? Why?" I closed the door and clutched the towel tighter to my chest.

"I went downstairs to look for you when you weren't in your room. She actually made me eat breakfast with her."

Yeah, I'd stood quite a while under that shower. Since my mom seemed fine with him being in my room in spite of me being grounded, I relaxed. And soaked in the joy of seeing Tony this morning. He wore my favorite outfit—dark blue jeans, a cobalt blue tee, and an unbuttoned shirt over it. His feet dangled off my bed, bobbing up and down.

"Did Hunter come to apologize?"

My brows quirked as his casual tone dragged me out of my staring. "Sorry?"

"I saw him walk away from your house today. Bit early to come pay you a visit. So did he apologize for crawling into bed with you?"

Only then did I remember that I was in fact royally pissed at Tony. "I don't see how this is any of your concern. Anyway, it's early for you to be here, too." I folded my arms over my chest, but then the towel threatened to slide down. I returned to clutching it.

"Oh, come on..." He rose from the mattress and came toward me.

I backed away until the door behind me stopped me dead.

"I don't like it when you're mad at me." He gave that sweet, teasing pout he always did when he was trying to make me forgive whatever he screwed up. His playing with my wet strands of hair worked to crush my defenses. "To make it up to you we'll stay inside all day, and we can watch some movies."

Solidly united, just the two of us, like in the past.

He almost had me. But I decided to stay strong. With a snort, I slipped past him and strode to the closet, fetching a green t-shirt and jeans. Staring at the top for a couple seconds, I put it back. I wouldn't wear his favorite color today.

"I brought *X-Men*," he cooed and held the DVD collection in front of my face.

Oh, the bastard. He knew that was my all-time favorite. I owned the DVDs too, but he had the director's cut. I pressed my lips together. A grin still escaped.

Victory lit up his face. "You go dress, and I'll set the DVD player."

Faithful to his promise, Tony stayed the entire day. By the time we started on the second movie, I had forgiven him so much that I overcame the foot of distance between us on my bed and snuggled up to him. His arm, wrapped around my shoulders, brought back the familiar comfort. I wasn't sure if he noticed when he started winding a wisp of my hair around his finger, but I gloried in it.

There was just one thing bothering me all that time. I couldn't stop comparing the feeling with him to the sensation I'd felt when Ryan Hunter had rolled with me off the couch and I'd landed on top of him.

While now I was completely at ease, I had barely been able to reign in my fluttering heart in Ryan's tight embrace. How could that happen when I loved only Tony? Since I missed two thirds of part III of *X-Men* thinking on that question, I decided to drop the thought altogether. After all, Hunter wasn't a guy worth daydreaming about. *Right?*

The teasing smile he wore so well captured my mind once more.

Tony ruffled my bangs. "What? You still in love with the dude?"

"Bullshit! I'm not! It's just training!" The words were out before I could think as I jerked out of Tony's arm and glared at him.

He gave me a very uncomfortable stare. "What?"

"What—what?" *Shit.* Something had gone wrong. I sat back on my heels and chewed the inside of my cheek. "Sorry, what did you say?"

His eyes narrowed a little more. "You sighed. Like you were drooling over Hugh again."

Hugh…Jackman. Right. Not Hunter. A little late, my cheeks started to burn with shame.

"Liz, is everything all right?"

"Sure." And in my most innocent *I-don't-know-what-you-mean* voice I added, "Why?"

"Ever since I came back from camp you've been acting a little crazy."

"Bullcrap. I'm fine." The way he lounged on my bed, arms folded over his chest, brow creased, gave me the creeps. I slid off the bed and stopped the DVD. "Let's call it a day here, shall we?"

I held the case out to him, but Tony didn't take it. Instead, he sat up, Indian style, and angled his head. "Are you throwing me out?" He said it so slowly, disbelief flaring into his eyes.

Was I? In over thirteen years of friendship, I'd never asked him to go. Jeez, he was right—I was crazy.

"Look, I'm just tired from this movie marathon. And I promised my mom I'd clean up my room today." I dropped the DVD case on the bed in front of him. "It's almost four. I should get started."

"I'd offer to help you, but I've got this feeling you'll just say no." He stood, looking at me as if he was waiting for my contradiction.

What in the hell led me to disregard his offer? I avoided his gaze, finding his hoodie, and handed it over to him. "See you tomorrow?" A hopeful edge to my voice made me wonder if I was expecting him to be mad because I wouldn't let him help clean.

"Yeah. Meet you at practice. I can't pick you up,

though." He grimaced, and I wondered why. "But hey, tomorrow we're playing the first real match with the newbies. Make sure you play on my team." There it was again. The typical, sly Tony grin that caused my heart to melt every time.

Except it wasn't lopsided…like Hunter's.

I grunted, aware of my lack of focus, as I ushered Tony out of my room. As he climbed down the shed and I closed the window, I wondered where Mom kept the clinical thermometer. I must've been suffering from a high fever.

Chapter 9

Tuesday, two thirty P.M., I pedaled my mountain bike to the soccer field. Susan rode along with me, and we were the last to arrive. After securing my bike, my gaze swept over the trimmed lawn in search of Tony. He stood on the far end with a small group of girls and boys. I started toward him, but when one of his friends headed away, I glimpsed Chloe there and decided to skip their doubtlessly *entertaining* conversation.

It didn't take long for Tony to spot me and excuse himself from the group. Barbie grabbed his biceps, saying something to him and pointing an eerie scowl in my direction. I glared back, feeling an overwhelming need to flip her off. But I was grown-up enough to resist.

Thankfully, I couldn't hear what she said to Tony; I was so not interested. But the fact that he rolled his eyes at her and pried her hand from his arm was highly satisfying.

He jogged over. "Hi, Liz. Are those shades new?"

Yeah, it was a good feeling that the guy knew my entire collection of clothes and accessories. It meant he paid attention. I grinned.

"Nope, they're mine," Hunter said behind me. When he came around to face me and carefully slid the sunglasses off my nose, I couldn't stop my smirk from spreading into a real smile.

"He gave them to me after the party," I told Tony, who suddenly looked a bit puzzled. "Hangover and sunlight—not a good combination."

Both boys laughed at that, and I had a hard time deciding which sound pleased me more.

As we headed toward the gathering group of kids, Ryan asked Tony if he wanted to be captain of the other scrimmage team.

"Sure. Want to pick players in turn?" Tony's eyes

skated over to me. A wink said I was one of his first choices.

"Yep, you can pick first," Ryan said to him then laid his arm over my shoulders. "But not her."

Stunned, I stopped, and I swore Tony stared at Hunter with the same look of amazement as I did.

Ryan ignored him. His arm slipped away from me, and the left side of his lips tilted up. "Play with me?"

Man, I lost my voice. Hunter knew how miserably I handled the ball. Still, he wanted me on his team.

Tony awaited my answer with a comical grin. Since he didn't seem annoyed at all, I thought I might as well accept. "*Okay.*" And yeah, if that hadn't come out so much like a question, I wouldn't have sounded like a total idiot.

"Cool. Let's play some ball, guys." Tony jogged ahead and had his first pick of players.

I didn't pay attention to who he called for his team, because Hunter asked me one basic question then. "Do you know how to play soccer, Matthews?"

"Kick the ball into the goal?"

He chuckled, rubbing his neck. "Yeah, that and a little more. For now, just don't touch the ball with your hands and try not to kick it past those white lines." He pointed at the rectangle marking the playing field.

"You know, I'm not a complete imbecile."

Or maybe I was. Before the first ten minutes were over, I'd hurt my wrist on the ball zooming toward me, and twice it went sailing far behind the opposite goal due to a kick of mine. Great. But on the plus side, no one shouted at me like Ryan did yesterday on the beach.

At least no one did until I apparently made the most fatal error of all when I aimed for a goal again.

"Offside," several guys shouted at once, some of them rolling their eyes.

I stood totally at a loss.

"Never mind. I'll explain this tomorrow," Ryan said as he came running toward me and kicked the ball to someone from Tony's team. He took his position on the field again, but not before he offered me a grin. "Nice shot."

He could try, but it didn't lift my spirits. Discouraged from the failures, I went to the far back, close to our own goal, deciding to be the passive player for the rest of the game. Except Hunter had a different idea. For some reason he kept me in the game, sending killer shots to me, spurring me on to give my best.

And I did. For three and a half minutes. Then I experienced, for the first time, how a kick against the shin felt. The pain, when Chloe's shoe collided with my leg, brought me to the ground. I bit my lip to stop my eyes from watering.

"Come on, guys! Play fair!" Ryan shouted. He stood over me and offered me his hand to pull me up. "You okay?"

I said nothing but nodded. My voice would have betrayed me otherwise. He sent me back into the game.

The pain from that little escapade wasn't completely gone when Chloe got me again. I cursed her in a volume loud enough to compete with a police siren, but it ricocheted off her thick head. When it happened a third time, I knew she was doing it on purpose. So from then on I didn't touch the ball, in order to not give her a reason to kill me out on the field.

After the game, Tony worked his fingers into the muscles at my neck as I hunched on the bench. "If I had known you're actually such a good player, I would have made you play with me every day after school."

I gave an irritated snort. His being nice did little to mend my broken pride—or bones. "That girl chose the wrong sport. She'd be a pro at kick-boxing."

"Who? Chloe?" At least this time, he didn't deny that she was after my life. "Did she get you bad?"

I scowled at him over my shoulder. "She was like an eighteen-wheeler."

He bit his lip. "She can be an aggressive player."

Which put it mildly. I sighed. "Are you going to hang here much longer? Because I really need to go home and tend to my bruised shin." And I was still grounded, of course.

The pause he took to scan the playing field made me wonder if he was looking for the troll with the bad temper. The flames of anger and jealousy licked up my spine. But she seemed to have gone already.

"I'm coming," he said.

On the way to our bikes, we crossed Ryan's path. He cut a brief glance to my leg and winced at the color. "Put ice on that ankle. I want you fit tomorrow."

The thought of more torture coming at me in just a few hours rendered me silent.

"What does he mean? There's no training with

the girls tomorrow. Just us guys," Tony pointed out as we walked on.

Okay, I figured it was time to spill. "Ryan is doing some personal training with me."

Tony could have said many things then, like asking me why, or where, or even when it was that I was insane enough to agree to that. But he chose to say the most stupid thing of all.

"With *you?*"

"Gee, thanks."

"Sorry, I didn't mean to sound like an ass. But...are we seriously talking about Hunter?" He snorted, and I should have kicked him in the butt for it.

"What's your problem with that?"

"No problem." He mounted his bike, waiting for me to get the number combination of my lock right. "Just thought you were grounded."

"I am."

"And you get out of the house for the training how?"

Now I avoided his gaze, jumping onto the pedals at a stand to get ahead of him. "Same way you get in."

He had no trouble catching up with me. "You're sneaking out? For *Ryan Hunter?*" If Tony was implying that I never did it for him, he let that leak from every syllable.

"So what?"

Tony cast me a sideways glance, his lips tight in a weak attempt at hiding a grin. "Here I'm gone for just a few weeks, and you turn into quite the teenage rebel." He laughs. "So, now that you're acquainted with the exclusive way in and out of your room, want to come to Charlie's for a drink with the others?"

"I'm not doing this during the day, Tony. My mom isn't *that* ignorant. Hunter picks me up at five in the morning," I whined. "He makes me run at the beach."

"Ah, fun guaranteed."

"I swear the guy is Satan in the flesh."

We reached my house, and while I got off my bike, Tony placed one foot on the pavement and studied me with those intense blue eyes. "You know I still don't get it. Why are you torturing yourself for a sport you've loathed all your life?"

"I never loathed soccer."

"You said it was the fifth, never-mentioned plague that would bring the world down."

Did I really say that? Wow, the man was good.

As I wheeled my bike into the shed, Tony's raised

voice drifted to me. "Is Hunter the reason?"

I froze, staring at Dad's fishing rods for an infinite moment. A pissed glare on my face, I finally walked outside, slowly, then leaned against the doorframe with my arms folded over my chest. "What in the world makes you think that?"

Tony had propped his forearms on the handlebar of his bike, leaning forward in a casual way. "Well, you two are pretty close lately."

Okay, I was almost seventeen, had never been kissed, and I'd had all I was going to take from my best friend. "Are you really that ignorant? I'm *not* doing this for Hunter."

"Then why?"

Christ forgive me, I was going to slap him in a moment. "I'm doing this because of you!"

My heart stopped the moment I understood my slip.

Tony's mouth hung open as he stared at me. He gripped the metal of the handlebar, closing his fingers so hard the white showed around the knuckles. Not quite the reaction I had prayed for the past five or so years.

His gaze dropped, his eyes trained on the ground in front of him. That was an eerie moment. Heck, I didn't think something could shock Tony so much. Anything. Especially me. Okay, the hope that he would be all smiles and kiss me for my almost-declaration of love had slipped with his look, but his stunned silence made me feel very uncomfortable. I wished I was a snowman and could melt right now.

"Come here, Lisa," he finally said.

No. I waited a couple of seconds, struggling to get rid of the panic setting in. When I didn't obey, he stepped off his bike and came toward me, the slowness only adding to my anxiety.

"Look—"

I shook my head, begging him to stop. "Please don't give me that shit of *you're like my sister* now."

"I won't. Because we both know you're far closer than that."

Oh my God, this was going downhill, and there was nothing to stop the avalanche I had kicked loose. My knees shook all of a sudden, my mouth went dry.

Tony reached out but stopped before he would touch my cheek. His lips pressed together, he withdrew his hand. "I'm dating Chloe."

What? No. Not that girl. Not any girl! No!

In deliberate movements, I backed off then walked into the house, not saying a word. With the screaming pain inside my soul, I quietly closed the door. It was all I could do not to break out in tears in front of Tony.

I couldn't breathe. My stomach knotted, making me sick. As the first tears started to fall, I flew into my bathroom and dry-heaved into the toilet.

Tony shouldn't see me like this, ever. I wished I could say he understood and that's why he didn't follow me. But with everything that had happened, I knew he probably just didn't want to face me after I'd declared my feelings for him.

It took hours until I could breathe again without my throat constricting and aching. I sat on my bed, flipping through the many photo albums I had made of us over the years. Each time I turned a page, I wanted to rage and cry again about the loss that ripped my insides apart. But I had shed all the tears I was capable of. I felt completely empty. Hollow. Alone.

When Mom called me to dinner and I told her I wasn't hungry, she tried in her understanding way to make me talk. I had a hard time convincing her that I just wanted to be left alone. In the end she let me be, and I locked myself in my room. In my personal realm of misery.

As the sun set and I slumped on my bed with some heavy rave music on the iPod, I faced another problem.

I wasn't going to play soccer anymore. Ever. And I needed to cancel on Hunter's training the next day.

I called Simone and got his cell phone number, but I wasn't in the mood to talk to anyone, so I sent him a text.

Me

Don't need to train tomorrow. And I want off the team. Lisa

But then, as far as I knew, he only knew my last name, so I added *Matthews* in parentheses.

It didn't take long for my message to be answered.

Ryan

Does it hurt that much?

What kind of question was that? The pain eating my insides was killing me. I slammed the phone on the nightstand and dropped onto my pillow with a snort. Seconds later, I realized he actually had no idea what had happened. *He must mean something else. Of course—my leg.* Palm pressed to my brow, I breathed deep.

Me

No, leg is fine. I'm just done with soccer. Thanks for your help. Bye

I expected him to accept that and leave me alone. He did…for fifteen minutes. Then the next message came.

Ryan

Okay. Talked to Mitchell. So the cat's out?

The cat's out? Seriously? What the hell—Ryan knew about them dating and didn't tell me? But then, what reason would he have had? We weren't really friends, and he didn't know about my love for Tony.

Or maybe he did. M&M. Everyone knew it. I felt so terribly exposed right then. The entire town knew about my obsession with this boy, while he was dating this bimbo. The urge to cry again persisted, but no tears fell. So I turned up the volume of the music and tried to blast my brains into oblivion with it.

The phone vibrated on the mattress next to me.

Ryan
Can you slip out after dark?

Me
I probably could. But why would I do that?

Ryan
Distraction ☺

I wasn't in the mood to be distracted. Not in any mood at all, actually. I only wanted to wallow in self-pity.

Me
Really, I'm not up for more torture.

God, if only the world would leave me alone for the next few hours. But no such luck. As soon as darkness fell, a low voice carried up to my room. "Get down here, Matthews!"

I choked on the piece of chocolate I'd just shoved into my mouth. I rubbed my tears-sticky eyes and rushed to the window. "Why did you come? Can't you read? I said no."

"You said *no torturing you.* I'm not going to. Now get into some nice clothes, wash your face, and come out."

"I'm not in the mood—"

He jumped and climbed onto the roof of our shed then stalked toward my window with this evil grin on his lips.

Chapter 10

"May I come in?" Hunter didn't wait for my reply but ducked through the window frame and entered my personal domain.

I sucked in a breath and stumbled backward. The bed stopped me, catching my fall.

"Nice room." Hands braced on the edge, Ryan sat on the sill. "*You* look miserable."

"Gee, thanks for the news update."

He lifted his ball cap and raked a hand through his hair, his lips tightening. "Listen, I totally suck at this whole *want-to-talk-about-it* crap."

"Then why are you here?"

He shrugged. "Perhaps because I'm good at having fun and taking your mind off certain things. So what do you say? Want to come party a little?"

Another party with Ryan? Images of lying in his bed, my leg wrapped around his, flashed in my memory. "I think I'll stay home and listen to some music instead."

He grimaced. "Don't do this to yourself. No guy is worth it." Then he did something I least expected. He walked toward me, took both my hands, and gently pulled me off my bed. "Come on, *Lisa.*"

My name from Ryan Hunter. That was a first. And it sounded incredibly nice.

"I really don't know—"

"I do. And now stop arguing." He gave me a few seconds to stare into his deep brown eyes and make up my mind.

I released a long breath. "Can I shower first?"

"Oh, please do that." He dropped onto my bed and found the photo albums that still sat there.

I grabbed them before he could and shot him a warning glare. "Don't touch anything."

He quirked his brows, lifting his palms in surrender. "Nothing," he promised. Then he added,

"Apart from your diary and maybe your lacy underwear."

God, I prayed I hadn't heard him right.

It took me twenty minutes to get ready to leave my room with Ryan—through the window.

This time he gripped my wrists in a tight lock and lowered me from the roof. He let me drop the remaining three feet, but that was okay. While he climbed down the tree Tony-style, I adjusted my snug-fit tee with the deep neckline. Dark blue jeans covered the bruises Tony's new girlfriend had left on my shins.

Ryan led me to a dark metallic-gray Audi-something parked on the curb. I didn't know much about cars, but enough to understand that his was modified. There was a lot less space between the low-slung car and the street than with a normal car. When I looked at its front with the strange headlights, only one word came up to describe the appearance. *Furious.*

Damn, that car looked hot enough to melt ice.

"Nice car," I offered.

"Thanks. You have your license?"

"Yeah, got it last summer."

"Want to try her out?"

"Why?" I laughed.

"Fun. And distraction." He shrugged, leaning an arm on the open door. "Unless you're chicken."

Grinning, I got into the driver's seat. "How fast does *she* go?"

A smirk tugged on his mouth. "I promise you'll never find out." The keys jingled as he tossed them into my lap.

First I had to adjust the seat to my much smaller stature.

Ryan climbed in on the other side. "Think you can handle manual?"

My dad's car was a stick shift, so that wasn't a problem for me. I grinned, started the engine, and reversed out of the parking spot. The steering wheel was smaller than ours and took a few moments to get used to. But then we were off, and I raced the baby down to the beach in record time.

"Is that all you can do?" Ryan teased with a look at the speedometer.

I considered telling him that I'd gotten a ticket for speeding not long ago. But then I figured, why should my first bit of fun after such a horrid day be cut short?

Since he assured me the car would stick to the

asphalt, no matter how fast I went, I pushed down on the accelerator. It was amazing. The power, the speed, the purr of the engine. I laughed as I took a curve at a speed that would have carried my parents' car off the road. Hunter's Audi didn't budge an inch.

"Have you ever been to Club Tuscany?"

I cut him the briefest sideways glance, concentrating on that small part of the road that was brightened by the headlights at this killer speed. "I'm sixteen for another few weeks. Of course not."

"Ah, right."

That he sounded surprised made me a little uncomfortable. "How old are you?"

"Eighteen."

"Since when?" I blurted out.

"Last month."

Yeah, it made sense. Ryan was now a senior. "But that's still not old enough to go clubbing."

"It is when your brother-in-law owns the club." He smirked at me then pulled his ball cap lower down his forehead and scooted deeper into the seat. "Follow that road for another ten miles."

I did, feeling the rush of adrenaline streaming through my system. Everything about him was so dangerous. And I happened to enjoy that. Especially tonight.

A few minutes later, he gave me directions on which road to take and where to park the car. I climbed out to stand face-to-face with a bald bouncer who blocked the entrance to a square building painted dark red. "Club Tuscany" was spelled in huge beaming letters across the second-floor level.

"You need to wait till you turn twenty-one to get in, sweetness," the burly man said. I backed off instantly.

Ryan came around the car, caught me, and with his arm draped around my shoulders he moved me forward again. "Hi, Paul. She's with me. Is Rachel in tonight?"

"Hey, Ryan. Didn't know you were coming. Rachel won't be in until later, but Philip's here."

"Cool." He gave the bouncer a knuckle-pound then led me through the heavy, gray metal door Paul held open for us.

"Is Rachel your sister?" I whispered.

"Yeah. Philip is her husband. He's cool. You'll like him."

Thumps of a stomping beat drifted to us, growing louder with each step we took down the narrow aisle. I became hesitant, pulling on Ryan's arm to stop him.

"I don't think I should be here. On second thought, you shouldn't be here either."

"You worry too much. I'm here almost every weekend. Everyone knows me. And no one will bother you," he added as he dragged me with him.

Another door opened at his push. We entered a huge place tainted in blue light, brimming with people and smelling of dry smoke coming out of a smoke machine. A strobe light on the dance floor created a robotic atmosphere as people jumped to the music and bodies ground against each other.

Ryan rolled up the sleeves of his white shirt, then took my hand and pulled me toward the bumping mass. "C'mon, let's dance."

Heck, I wasn't a dancer. Protest was useless, because he wouldn't hear me shout in this club unless I plastered myself against him and yelled in his ear. I followed. He didn't stop until we stood in the middle of the dancing crowd.

My hand was captured in his, maybe because he knew I would have fled otherwise. Ryan moved closer, his free hand planted in the small of my back. "Loosen up, Matthews. You're supposed to be having fun." He pressed his lips to my ear to speak. "Or at least look like you are."

He gave me a soft push and made me twirl under his arm. Ryan did things so nonchalantly. The lightness of his demeanor, his unconcern, rubbed off on me at this moment. I laughed as he caught me again in an easy hug and swayed with me to the music. The dry smoke troubled my breathing a little, but this close to Ryan, all I smelled was him. And he smelled fantastic. Just like the other morning when I woke up next to him.

I didn't know what brought him to my house tonight. Could be he just felt pity for me for what had happened with Tony, and as the captain of our team, he made it his duty to cheer me up. Or he simply liked me. Whichever, I was thankful he hadn't given up when I told him no in the text message. Because he was a wonderful lift for my mood. He made me forget. He made me smile.

And right now he made me a little nervous.

I felt this tingle in my stomach every time I was close to him. Especially as he twirled me around and caught my back against his chest. His hand splayed on my belly, he pushed me against him, performing a body wave with me.

I laughed out loud, maybe to cover my shyness. "What are you doing?" I shouted over my shoulder and found his face very close to mine.

"Distracting you." He rolled again, and I felt each of his hard muscles grinding against my back. "Is it working?"

Unbelievably so. I didn't reply but let Ryan move me. With all the dancing, my tee was a mess, and the hem traveled up a few inches. Half of Ryan's hand lay on my naked stomach. It sent a shiver down my spine. One of the good ones.

As the song ended, he released me and shouted next to my ear, "Phil just came in. Let's say hello."

I smoothed my clothes out on the way to the oblong bar. The music wasn't as loud back there. Leaning over the metal top, Ryan introduced me to a man with shoulder-length hair and a black muscle shirt. He looked mid-thirties, maybe a bit younger. Phil set two cans of Coke in front of us.

After the hot dance with Ryan, this was more than welcome.

Perched on a bar stool, I listened while the two talked about Ryan's last year in high school and the new soccer team. Phil asked me if I liked it.

I lied. "Yeah, it's great. Love the training."

The slanted look from Ryan promised he didn't buy one word of it.

"What?" I mouthed at him with a half-smile.

He leaned in closer and brushed my hair behind my ear. "I still have the text where you say you're done with soccer, *Lisa.*"

The taunt in his voice as he said my name prickled my skin. I leaned back an inch so I could gaze at his face. "Did you really not know my name before I sent you that message?"

He laughed and shrugged one shoulder. "Why, Matthews? You were devoted to Mitchell. What would I care?"

From the way he averted his eyes for a second, and the sly grin that remained on his lips, I wasn't sure if I should believe him.

"You're such an ass, you know." I shoved his shoulder, grinning at him.

The roguish gleam in his eyes captured me. "I've been told girls go for that." He winked then drank from his Coke, but his gaze held mine all that time.

Heat rushed to my cheeks, because, hands down, he was right. It was all too easy to fall for him. Not only because he looked illegally good in a white shirt, or because of his amazing smell. It was the attention he gave me that made me feel good around him. Special. Desired, even.

And for the weirdest moment, I wanted him to desire me.

Letting my gaze slide to a few people who'd started singing karaoke on a small stage across the room, I hoped I could flush that idea with a long drink from my soda, deeming it a side effect of the pain Tony had caused me today. I wanted to stay faithful to my love for him, even if he made it clear that he'd rather kiss the Barbie clone than me. But with Hunter standing between my legs, his hand placed casually just above my right knee, it was no use denying the attraction. His charm had worked on me for days now, and it was different to anything I had experienced so far. Fresh, exciting, dangerous. Nothing compared to good old *safe* Tony.

I wouldn't want them to switch places right now. And that was the scariest thought of all.

A tall, dark-haired beauty came up behind Ryan and dragged me out of my musing. She wrapped one arm around his neck and kissed him on the cheek. "Hi, little brother."

"Hey, Rach." He let her come around and introduced us.

As he called me *Matthews* and *the friend of a friend*, my heart sank. I reached out to shake Rachel's hand. "My name is Lisa."

"Don't mind him. The oaf was never comfortable with first names." The tall girl laughed and shoved her brother playfully. "I'm lucky—I'm his sister."

"That doesn't mean a thing, *Carter,*" he teased her and popped open another soda then clinked cans with Philip.

"So, the friend of a friend, huh?" Rachel's tone was light but curious. "Where is that friend?"

"Not here." Ryan grinned at her. It was hard to miss the certain glint of mischief in his eyes. The glint that didn't fail to make me nervous again as his gaze met mine.

Rachel sighed with a roll of her eyes. "Just when will you grow up and settle for *one?*"

"He's young, baby." Phil leaned over the counter to kiss his wife. "He has time."

"I know." She pulled away and snorted as she cast her brother a grin. "I'm just waiting for the day that a girl sees through you...and decides to like you anyway."

Ryan laughed. "Yep, me too."

After hiding from his mom in his parents' beach house yesterday, it was odd to see him banter with his family like that. Free, uncomplicated. Funny.

"That calls for a drink." Philip fetched two small glasses from behind the bar, placed one in front of himself and the other in front of Ryan, and started filling them with tequila.

"You can have your drink with Rach. I'll skip tonight." Ryan shoved the glass toward his sister, his lips suddenly getting a little too tight.

"You pass? With that beautiful drinking partner?" Philip's beam my way confused me. I didn't intend to drink a teeny tiny drop of that shit, but he hadn't given me a glass anyway, so what did he mean?

"I'm not having this drink with *her.*"

Okay, now Ryan's implications hurt. He would drink with other girls, but not with me?

"Why? Is she shy?" Phil demanded.

"She's too nice."

"Ah, she's a prude then."

What bullcrap was that? "I'm not a prude! And I'm standing right beside you, so I would appreciate it if you told me what the hell you're talking about."

Ryan turned a sheepish grin on me. He brushed his knuckle across my cheek. "She's decent," he told Phil.

"Yeah, and decent is a shit word for prude," I muttered. "So why don't you want to do with me whatever you are used to doing with other girls when you come here?" Somehow I felt that my hurt pride would land me in trouble. Still, I couldn't let them get away with calling me a prude. After all, I'd slipped out of my room twice for this guy while grounded. And currently I sat on a barstool in a club that opened its doors only for people aged twenty-one and over.

"You don't know what you're asking for, Matthews."

"Well, it won't kill me to find out, right?" God, I should bite off my tongue.

"Okay," Ryan drawled. "Remember, I gave you fair warning."

Chapter 11

Lips pressed together, I stared Hunter down, but with his last words he had me practically wetting my pants.

Philip, however, seemed pleased with the situation as he filled the two glasses—Ryan's only half-full at his sister's demand—with tequila and placed half of a lime slice on either one.

Ryan arched his eyebrows. "You still game?"

"I don't have to drink this, do I?" *Shit.* My voice almost cracked with my rising unease.

"No, you don't. That's for me. You only assist with the lime."

Assist with the lime…meant what? Feed it to him? Okay. I could do that. "Game on."

He cast me a smirk that made me wonder if I was in the right place at the right time. But it was too late to cop out. He took the lime off the tequila and clinked his glass to Philip's. At the same time he held the slice out to me. "Bite."

"What?"

"*Bite*," he repeated.

He dragged the brim of his cap around to the back of his head then knocked the shot down. I leaned forward and bit into the fruit he held out, my eyes trained on his face. Yuck, the sour taste made me grimace. I pulled back. Ryan tossed the slice away and cupped my neck, yanking me toward him. Everything happened so fast, I couldn't even lick the lime juice from my lips.

But he did. And my heart stopped beating.

He traced my bottom lip with his tongue, catching the juice there, and gave it a gentle nip. His tongue then delved in between my parted lips and slid against mine with a sensual slowness that sent little electric shockwaves of pleasure to the very tips of my fingers and toes.

The taste of liquor and lime stayed behind when

he drew back a few inches. His hand still on my neck, he gazed at me with something close to an apology in his eyes. That and satisfaction.

Me? I probably looked like a cat that was thrown into cold water. Stunned to the point where no sound came over my lips.

"Thanks for your help with the lime," he said in a voice so low I had to lip-read.

I breathed in slowly, but my heart was racing. "Uh-huh. Anytime."

My bafflement and dropped-open mouth fueled his amusement. Ryan cocked his head, close to letting go of the grin he bit down. Eventually, his hand slipped away from my neck and he turned to his brother-in-law but kept me close to him.

Rachel caught my stunned face and offered me her compassion with a sheepish shrug. She skirted her brother and engaged me in a conversation that didn't give me much time to breathe. Not quite what I wanted to do now while Hunter's taste in my mouth was all I could think about. But that woman was insatiable. She wanted to know everything about me, even what I liked for breakfast.

"She's the devil in disguise, hunting for potential in-laws. Don't let her make you sign anything," Ryan said over my shoulder, and I caught the spark in his eyes as he reminded me of the marriage license his parents seemed to request from any female visitors to their beach house. I shuddered but laughed when Rachel slapped him on the shoulder for that remark.

"Let me save you from the Spanish Inquisition." He grabbed my hand, pulling me off the bar stool and giving me no chance to object. But then, everything was fine with me as long as I didn't have to answer more questions. Or so I thought until I realized where exactly Hunter was dragging me.

"You're kidding me, right?" I resisted against his pull and made him stop just in front of the stage.

He smirked over his shoulder. "Nope."

My hands started to shake as he ushered me up the steps. He released me to talk to the guy behind the mixing desk. The song filling the bar stopped, the silence eerily frightening. I broke into a panic, sweat dotting my brow. Mouth dry and throat tight, I turned around and faced the crowd. The club suddenly appeared ten times bigger than when we had come in, with thousands more people…all staring at me.

Oh. My. God.

No way in hell was I going to sing in front of

them all. Grabbing onto what remained of my sanity, my gaze darted to the stairs, and I started toward them. But Ryan's arms caught me around the waist, and he dragged me to the microphone. Paralyzed, I couldn't even fight him.

"You're so going to pay for this," I hissed, feeling the rattle of my bones.

He laughed into my ear, enjoying himself. "You can hate me later. Now, we sing."

The music set off with a stomping beat. I recognized the melody immediately, slightly relieved I knew this remix of the old song by heart. A few seconds into the melody, Ryan blared into the mike, *"Almost heaven…West Virginia…"*

I didn't.

I just stood there, poker-stiff, and gaped at him, not believing he was really doing this to me. I wanted to kick him, slap him, shout at him, and I was sure he read it all in my horrified face. But what did he do? Held the mike in front of my lips. I had no choice but to sing "Country Roads" with him if I didn't want to end up a complete idiot in front of the crowd. So…I sang.

My voice boomed from the speakers overhead. Granted, it didn't sound all that bad. Ryan's grin spread wider as he kept singing the lines with me. And I found I could keep my voice steady and walk through the text as long as I focused on his encouraging eyes. When the song picked up pace, I even felt a grin on my lips. Weird, but with the seconds ticking by, and me not screwing up, I was starting to enjoy it.

Not long, and the crowd was singing with us.

From the cool way Ryan handled this, moving his body lightly with the rhythm, stomping his heel, I wondered how many times he'd been standing up here in the past. Damn, he looked incredibly sexy as he sang and danced to the music.

Suddenly, he left me alone with the microphone. My newfound courage dropped to the ground in a second, together with my stomach. I followed him with my eyes as he moved behind me and I continued with the song. Taking my hands, he raised them above my head and clapped them to the beat. The crowd followed suit, singing and cheering us on. It was amazing.

The warmth of his body pressed against my back gave me the feeling of safety again. I heard his voice in my ear as he sang with me, but the rest of the club would only hear me. I still hated him. But I had to admit it was fun all the same. And I smiled.

Finally, the song was over. I struggled to breathe evenly and rubbed the sweat off my forehead. Whistles and shouts encouraged us to perform another song.

Ryan flashed a tempting grin. "What do you think?"

"I think I'm going to kill you." I laughed. "No way are we doing this again." This time I gave him no choice. I grabbed his hand and pulled him off the stage with me.

Rachel had joined her husband behind the bar, his arms wrapped around her waist as both watched us approaching. "That was awesome," she said, beaming at me. "You'd really make a sweet couple."

After the horror he'd made me go through? "Yeah, right." I laughed. Too loud, still surfing on an adrenaline high. I glanced at my wristwatch and decided a quarter to midnight was a good time to go home. We said goodbye to Ryan's family and headed out to his car.

The cool air felt wonderful on my face. I pressed my hands to my burning cheeks.

"Want to drive again?"

I turned to him, my knees still a little wobbly. "I

think I'll pass. The way I feel right now I might very well wrap your car around a tree."

Grinning, he laid his arm around my shoulders and walked me to the passenger side. He held the door open for me.

Streetlamps illuminated the car's inside in beacon-like intervals as he brought me home at a casual cruise. I watched the lamps travel by my window for a while, then tilted my head the other way and studied Ryan driving, which was a far more captivating sight.

He responded with a brief glance my way. "Did you enjoy yourself tonight?"

I'd definitely enjoyed him. "It was okay." I shrugged, but then I bit my lip and decided I could give him something closer to the truth. Through a snarky grin, I added, "Actually, it was quite nice. But I still hate you!"

"I know." His chuckle resounded in the cabin. "I'm sorry I dragged you into hell on that stage."

"And you *should* be."

As the headlights of another car broke through the windshield, his brows knitted slightly. He waited till the street was ours alone again then probed, "What about the lime surprise?"

"What about it?"

"Should I be sorry about that, too?"

Him being sorry that he was my first kiss? Warmth flowed through me when I remembered how soft his lips felt. A good thing he couldn't see my body tense in reaction. I tried for a casual tone. "Nah. I just should have heeded your warning."

"Yeah." An impish flash crossed his eyes. "Or maybe…just not."

"Or maybe not…" I agreed, feeling the heat conquering my face.

"You liked it?" On the straight road, he shot me a quick glance, teasing me with his beguiling half-smile. I didn't respond, so he faced front again and chuckled softly. "Yeah, you did."

My lips twitched. I rolled my head back to the window side and decided to keep my thoughts to myself.

Ryan stopped the car a few houses away from mine in order to not give me away to my parents. As he walked me home, I noticed the shimmer of light in Tony's room and wondered what he'd done tonight to still be up. But then, it wasn't my business, like I had learned this afternoon. I forced my thoughts in another direction. Ryan Hunter's way.

He made me smile the way he watched me as we walked. In front of our shed, he braced himself, feet planted firmly on the ground. I knew I was going to be catapulted up to the roof again, and I so didn't like it.

"What do you say, Matthews? Shall we do this again sometime?"

Partying until midnight? "Maybe we should. But let's wait until my detention is over. I really hate sneaking in and out like a criminal."

He laughed quietly and hoisted me onto the shed. A moan pushed out of my lungs as I landed on my stomach and dragged myself further up, swinging my legs over the edge. Yeah, agility and I had nothing in common.

"Good night," I whispered on the way to my room.

"Later 'gator."

I slipped inside and grabbed my boy shorts and tank top, thinking of this day and how weird it turned out in the end. Kissed by Ryan Hunter. That was crazy. I was totally in love with Tony, and yet I ran my tongue over my lips dreaming of Ryan's beautiful tiger eyes.

Heck, was he thinking of me right now too?

With a long dreamy sigh, I sprawled on my bed, reaching for the lamp on my nightstand. But as soon as the light went out, a rustle in the tree and then footsteps on the roof of the shed made me switch it back on. My heart kick-started in my chest. This could only be Tony. He must have seen me come home. And I wasn't sure if I really wanted to see him right now. Not just because I was still hurt about him dating the bimbo. But because I'd much rather have seen someone else again—with the sexy brown eyes. Ah damn. I crawled out of bed and rubbed my temples that had suddenly started to hurt.

And then he was there, sitting on my windowsill, lifting his legs through. I swallowed hard, taking a barefooted step back.

"Hunter. What are *you* doing here?"

Chapter 12

"I forgot something."

"You can't just come up here. I'm already in my jammies." My protest was weak like a moth's wing-beat. In fact, I couldn't care less about my current clothing. All that mattered was that he was here. A burst of adrenaline swept through me.

Ryan walked toward me with this predatory look and a sly grin. His gaze skated down my bare legs. Shivers left a trail of goose bumps on my skin. "I've never seen anything sexier than those shorts on you."

He blasted the rest of the world right out of my

mind when he hooked his finger in my waistband and pulled me closer. My hands came up to rest on his chest. Stunned, I gaped at him, my eyes wide.

This was too close. But I couldn't stop staring at him, at his lips... Screw Tony and my preserved love for him.

"You forgot something?" Shit, I sounded more like a toad than myself. "What?"

Ryan took off his ball cap and tossed it on my bed. His hand moved around my waist, pulling me even closer, his other palm shaped against my cheek and neck. He leaned in so slowly that I thought I was going to die of anticipation. His gaze moved to my lips and back to my eyes. He dipped his head.

The first soft touch of his lips to mine rendered my eyes shut. I let him hold me, guide me, work my mouth open with his kiss. A little shy, I shifted my hands up and around his neck. He seemed to enjoy that because he pressed me harder against him. My breasts got squeezed between us. His tongue brushed against mine, very slightly at first. The intimacy of this move had me shaking to my core.

Ryan thrust his hand into my hair. As he deepened the kiss, I finally responded with a surprising moan. I let him engage me in a dance of lips and tongues, sometimes eager, and then soft the next moment. The wonderful musky smell of his aftershave filled my head, and I knew the scent would be etched in my mind forever with the memory of him rocking my world tonight.

He inched away and waited for me to open my eyes. With a half-smile, he leaned his brow against mine. "By the way, I've known your name since the very day you first came to watch Mitchell's soccer practice in ninth grade, Lisa."

I bit down a grin at his surprising confession. "Have you, really?"

His lips thinned to a mocking line. "Mm-hm." He nudged my nose with the tip of his then took my mouth again in a beguiling, slow kiss. His hands started to explore underneath my top, skimming the sensitive skin along my spine.

I surrendered to him, my knees getting weaker with the heat he ignited inside me, but he supported part of my weight with a tight embrace.

"What the fucking hell—!"

Ryan was pulled away from me so fast I had no chance to protest other than with a grunt, struggling to keep my stance.

"Take your bloody hands off her!"

"No! Tony!" A strangled shriek escaped me as he punched Ryan hard in the jaw.

Ohmygod! Ohmygod! Ohmygod!

Ryan staggered back a step then caught himself before he crashed into my closet. I rushed to him, but he held his hand out and stopped me with a scowl that turned my blood cold. He ran his tongue over his cut lip then wiped the blood off with the back of his hand. The next instant he had Tony pinned against the wall, with his forearm pressed to Tony's throat.

"I'll let you off this one time because you're my *friend*, Mitchell," he growled as dangerously as a rabid wolf. "But do that again and you won't live through the night."

"You don't scare me, Hunter."

I had never seen Tony so furious. He didn't heed Ryan's warning, but head-butted him in the nose. My mind roared in panic. I couldn't move, caught in a stranglehold of shock. From the edge in Ryan's eyes as he clamped his teeth, I could tell Tony had just signed his own death sentence.

Full of fear for my best friend and no less sorry for Ryan's bleeding nose, I struggled to get a grip and stepped between them, one hand braced on either of their chests. "No. *No!* You're not going to do this.

Not in my room," I hissed. "And not over me." Then I scowled at them both in turn with the insane fear my parents would wake up and kill me for having two boys in my room in the dead of the night.

When I wouldn't let them get at each other, both drew in a deep breath, and the rattle of my bones from holding them back eased a little. I turned to Tony, staking him with the horror I felt. "Why did you come here?" *And ruin the most beautiful moment of my life. You idiot!*

"I had to make sure this asshole keeps his hands off your body."

Ryan glared at him over my outstretched arm. Unlike Tony, he was amazingly calm, which just freaked me out all the more. "You've chosen one helluva moment to show up."

"Seems like I'm just in time. You're not going to touch her again."

"I'm sure Lisa can speak for herself and doesn't need *you* to babysit her." With those words, Ryan placed his hands on my hips and moved me to the side.

I wasn't sure if this was a good idea, but with Tony being so furious, I somehow appreciated not being in his way anymore. Ryan took a protective stance beside me and nailed Tony with a hard look. "This is none of your business."

"She's my friend and sure as hell *is* my business," Tony spat.

"What's your problem, man?"

"You are. This shit ends now. I didn't ask you to go that far with her."

Ryan stiffened. "Shut the hell up, Mitchell," he warned in a voice gone lethal.

But suddenly I didn't want Tony to shut up. In fact I wanted to know what he meant.

Taking a provocative step toward him, he continued. "I didn't mean for you to sleep with her when I asked you to distract her."

At his words, my stomach churned.

This was too much information for just two seconds. Finding Ryan's shocked face, I narrowed my eyes. "Distract?" No real sound came out of my mouth. I had heard that word one too many times tonight.

Lips tight, his jaw hardened. "It's not like that—"

"No?" Then what? The club, the kiss. Him letting me drive his car. It was all part of his brilliant plan to *distract* me. And he was sent by Tony who just wanted to feel better—do a good deed for the old friend he'd hurt. I wanted to curl up on the floor and bawl at the unfairness of my life.

"Bullshit, of course it's like that," Tony answered before Ryan could say more. "He called me this afternoon, wanting to know why you'd quit soccer all of a sudden. I asked him to get your mind off…well—" He looked at me, shamefaced, but his voice became softer. "Off *us*. I knew you didn't want to see me, but I couldn't stand the thought of you being in your room all alone, crying." Then his tone hardened twice as much as it had before. "But now that I think of it, it was a crappy idea from the beginning. You deserve better than him. All he wants is to get in your pants. Don't you, Hunter?"

Wait. "I deserve better?" I couldn't believe he'd say something as trite as that when he'd been the one to choose Barbie girl over me. "Then who, Tony? *You*?" Cynicism leaked from every syllable.

"I was good enough for you for the past ten years."

You were. Until this afternoon, when you ripped my heart right out of my chest.

Ryan shoved Tony away and stared him down, venom seeping through his glare. "*Now* you start to fight for her? You goddamned idiot!"

"I don't have to fight for her. Not with you. She never wanted you."

"She might, now. And that scares the shit out of you, doesn't it? Giving her up, but not wanting her to be with someone else. You're pathetic."

If I looked at it that way, he really was. But what in the world had happened that I suddenly had two furious guys fighting over me in my room? This couldn't be true. I searched Tony's face. "What's going on? You told me you're dating Chloe. So why are you in my room in the middle of the night?"

He shot me a glance that said he'd rather not talk with Hunter in the room. A very queasy feeling rose in my gut. Instinctively, I grabbed the edge of my desk for support.

"Not hard to guess," Ryan answered my question, but he kept his eyes pinned on Tony. "You slept with Chloe. And she dumped you like I told you she would, didn't she?"

Tony was silent.

He. And Chloe. Naked. In *one* bed.

A scream started in my head that threatened to shatter my ears from the inside. My knees gave way, and I collapsed on the bed. Tony reached for me, but I spider-crawled away from him, my throat hurting as

I forced air into my lungs. "Don't you dare touch me!"

He planted one knee on the mattress. "Please, Liz—"

"No!" I slapped him—for the first time ever—and his head jerked sideways with the force of my palm. "Just go!"

Tony breathed a few times, keeping me in focus, jaw hardening. I felt he wasn't going to give up, so I narrowed my eyes, filled with all the spite and coldness I was capable of. *"Now!"*

With that, he finally backed off. He puffed a frustrated grunt and climbed out through the window. We both knew that one day we would talk again, but I'd decided that day was a long way ahead.

Ryan watched him silently then turned to me, blood dripping from his nose and bottom lip. He wiped it off. A scarlet line trailed across the back of his hand. "I really didn't—"

"Stop it! I don't know which of you disgusts me more tonight." Tony, for what he did with Chloe when I still loved him. Or Hunter, who was just the ass I'd always suspected him to be, dragging me into something as beautiful as the kiss we'd shared when it was only for *distraction*. "Leave me alone. I'm done with you."

He wasn't the fool Tony had been to come for me with reassurances when I was close to losing it. But he took a damn lot longer to leave my room. I almost couldn't hold back my tears when I looked at his pleading eyes.

"I didn't come because Mitchell asked me to. I came because *I* wanted to see you again."

"Yeah, right. As if I would believe that. Distraction, huh? Tell me, did I look so miserable that you thought my life depended on your mercy?" I paused to swallow the hurt lodged like a hard ball in my throat. "Or did you really just want to get in my pants?"

Ryan pinched the spot between his eyes, the muscles in his jaw ticking violently. "Cut the crap, Lisa. You know that's not true."

The truth was, I didn't know what to believe anymore. My head ached too much to make sense of tonight. Right now, I wanted no one near me, especially not this liar. "Leave. I don't ever want to see you again."

Ryan didn't move for a solid minute. Then he came toward me, very slowly. Deliberately. He bent forward, planting his hands on the mattress on either side of me. He was right in my face, licking the blood off his lip. I didn't budge.

"For a minute there, I thought I stood a chance. But I guess in the end, Mitchell will still be the lucky one." He moved closer still and bridged the inch of gap between our faces. What the heck, coming in for a kiss? I sucked in a breath. But he reached past me for his cap and straightened, pulling the brim deep down over his brow. "See you around, Matthews."

Ryan didn't look back as he crossed to the window and disappeared into the dark.

Falling back on the mattress, I curled into a tight bundle and started sobbing into my pillow. Just where was the goddamned rewind button for today?

Chapter 13

Days passed, and I didn't hear from either of them. It was a long week. Too long, with too much thinking on my part. The thinking mostly focused on two specific moments. One, Ryan's delicious lips capturing mine. And two, Tony and Chloe, an image I just couldn't get out of my mind. After Tuesday night, I thought I wouldn't live through the pain that ripped open my heart like steel claws. But finally I fell into a state of numb indifference to not only Tony and Ryan, but also to the rest of the world.

By Friday, my mom rescinded my detention. She

said she had never seen so little of me in all her life, or how pale and withdrawn I had become, and it worried her. Yeah, my room was my castle. I didn't need food, or company. And I wasn't sure when I'd last had a bath.

Even without being grounded, I saw no particular reason for leaving my fort. Let the world go on without me, I didn't care. I was content with the one hundred and twenty square feet of this earth under my domain.

Saturday afternoon, the first text message came. From Tony.

Tony
Can I come up?

Since the day we'd decided to be best friends because we both loved *Tom and Jerry* cartoons, he'd never once asked before coming to my room, using either the door or my window. I sighed then walked to the open window with the cell phone in my hand. Tony was leaning against the tree, hands tucked into the pockets of his blue jeans. I wondered if he knew what he wore today, the blue tee and the shirt over it, was my favorite. And if he'd chosen it on purpose.

Our gazes met, and his face had the word sorry etched in every line. I didn't know what message my expression was sending him, but in case he didn't get it right, I slowly shut the window. To be absolutely clear, I pulled the curtains closed, too.

Funny, the same day, Ryan tried to call me. I didn't answer the phone, but decided to block his number so I wouldn't be tempted to pick up should he try again. I couldn't sleep all night then, because I wondered if blocking him was the right decision after all. Close to three in the morning, I cancelled the block. He'd tried to reach me two more times. There was also a text.

Ryan
Please talk to me!

For some reason, I really wanted to reply to that text. I missed him. Hoped he would be honest with me and could convince me he wasn't an ass after all. But I was scared he might do just that, and I'd be the idiot who believed him. So I sent one message back.

Me
Go to hell!

That, at three in the morning, was enough to render him silent. He didn't try to contact me again after that.

Fantastic. It seemed I'd gotten just what I wanted. Only I hated it.

A few days before school started again, Susan Miller called me. She wanted me to do some back-to-school shopping with her. I let her talk me into it in a thirty-minute phone call, and then only because I was curious how the soccer training was going since I'd opted out. Even more, I wanted to find out how things were between Ryan and Tony, and shopping with Susan was the perfect opportunity.

She picked me up on Friday morning, and we decided to take a walk to town instead of driving her father's car. In fact, this was the first time in weeks I made it past the borders of our garden and into civilization. It felt like I'd been gone from this world for years. So I was all the more surprised that nothing had changed.

"I've missed you at training," Susan confessed as we entered Staples. Then she made a gagging face. "Hunter let Millicent Kerns from his biology class on the team to replace you. I swear the girl is like an avalanche when she goes for the goal. Buries everything underneath her."

I grinned at that picture. One-hundred-and-sixty-pound Millicent was just the girl to roll across the field like a snow slide. While we rummaged through a box of pens and picked several notebooks, I said in the most nonchalant way, "Yeah, I kind of miss it, too. But after I hurt my leg the first time, I thought I'd better not do this murderous sport as a profession."

Susan dropped a pink pencil back into the box and slowly turned to stare at me, folding her skinny arms over her nonexistent breasts. "Are you shitting me?"

That grabbed my attention. I opened my mouth to say something, but I just didn't know what. So I closed it and gaped at her with quirked brows.

"Everyone knows you quit playing because Hunter put the moves on you, and you didn't like it."

I took a few moments to think this over. "Is that so?" *Who made up that bullshit?*

"Yeah. Well…it's the truth, isn't it?"

If I kept taking pauses between answering like I did, people might start to consider me a little slow. "Not exactly."

Her eyes narrowed. Little Susie seemed slightly confused. "What do you mean, *not exactly?* He didn't hit on you?"

"He did. I just meant the *'I didn't like it'* part."

"Wow, so you did?"

Like it? "Yeah, I think so."

Susan laughed as if this was the most pleasing news she'd heard in weeks. She grabbed a few notebooks and dropped them into her shopping basket. Then she stopped dead and turned to me, looking like she was about to explode. "Then why, for Pete's sake, did you leave the team?"

I played with the notebooks in my hand and shrugged. "It's a little complicated." And not something I wanted to talk about. Her eyes were boring into my head, so I sighed and decided to spill. "He kissed me, and I liked it, okay? Only, he didn't do it for the right reason. Not because he *really* liked me. More as a favor to a friend."

"Are you bananas, babe? Ryan Hunter is completely under your spell."

As she stressed every syllable, my chin dropped to my chest. "What?"

"Do you have any idea how long it took him to convince Tony to bring you to one of his parties?"

"You serious?"

She nodded vigorously. "And you were the only

one who made it on the team without scoring a goal at tryouts. I would know, I had to score two to really prove myself."

"Wait, that's not true. I hit Frederickson straight in the chest."

Susan's grin irritated me. "Do I need to lay the rules of soccer out for you? A goal is *not* where you hit the goalie."

Damn, she was right. "But Tony and Ryan told me to shoot at him."

"Because it was the easiest way for you to succeed."

I slapped my brow and ground my teeth. Ryan really had treated me in a favored way. But why would he?

As if to answer my silent questions, Susan tilted her head, pursed her lips, and sang in an annoying *I-told-you-so* tone, "He likes you."

"Yeah, maybe," I agreed in a low voice.

"So what are you going to do? Come back to play soccer?"

"No."

She made a pouty face. "Why not?"

"I told you, it's complicated."

"You're still in love with Tony. That's it, right?

M&M will never really break up."

At this point I regretted coming to town with Susan Miller, nag-queen of Grover Beach High. If she wasn't so sweet in her own nosy way, I'd have turned and walk out of the store already.

"I think it's cool that you forgave him. Chloesetta Summers was just a stupid mistake after all."

"Chloesetta?" I snorted with laughter at the name.

"The girls on the team call her that because she has the irritating ability to drag every boy into her closet and make out with them. I think the name fits."

Me too. However, I couldn't believe how much Susan knew about my private life. And with her, the entire soccer team it seemed. Maybe it was time to set a few facts straight. "I don't think Tony and I will ever be what we were before *Chloesetta* got hold of him."

Her nose wrinkled as she shifted her mouth funnily to one side. "Shame. You were like the only absolute in a changing world as we grew up."

It *was* a shame. But I didn't want our chat to go down this road. So I shrugged it off and dragged her to the cash register, where we waited in line to pay for our items. However, it didn't take long for curiosity got the best of me. "How are Tony and Hunter getting along during training, anyway? Last time I saw them, one had a bleeding nose."

"It's spooky. They either shout at each other, or they don't speak at all. No one who sees them now would believe they were *this close*"—she crossed her fingers for emphasis—"only a few weeks ago."

It hurt me in a strange way to hear that. I knew how much Tony idolized Ryan. Their friendship went way back. The thought that I had driven a wedge between them upset me to no end. And as this realization sank in, I knew I had forgiven him. He'd been a complete ass a few weeks ago, but he'd been my best friend for a lifetime. Maybe it was time to see him. Set things straight between us and repair our friendship if I could.

For all the nagging Susan did that afternoon, I was still glad I'd gone out with her. We said goodbye at my front door, but instead of going to my room, I tossed the bag with the books and pens on the shelf in the hallway and headed out again.

Wearing my spaghetti-strapped top, a humid evening breeze settled around my naked arms and shoulders as I walked the few steps between my house and Tony's. After not seeing him for so long, my heart thudded violently as I rang the doorbell.

Chapter 14

Eileen Mitchell answered the door.

"Hi, Mrs. Mitchell. Is Tony in?"

Her face, which had lit up when she saw me, now turned into an apologetic grimace. "Sorry, dear. You missed him by about ten minutes."

Perfect. Just my luck. "You wouldn't know where he went?"

Eileen shook her head. "Shall I send him over when he comes back?"

Should she? I grimaced. "No. I think I'll just call him."

She smiled and nodded, then closed the door as I dragged my feet from their front yard. I pulled out my phone, but somehow I didn't want to talk to him that way. So I punched in a text instead.

Me
Where are you?

Tony
Ground Zero

His answer came immediately. I hadn't even reached my front door yet.

My spirit lifted. I wheeled my bike out of the shed and pedaled it to the small lake where Tony and I had spent some very nice afternoons together. It wasn't really a lake, but more a pond in the middle of the woods. We used to call this place Ground Zero, because some ten years ago, Tony had found a strange box there, filled with six metal balls. He'd assured me they were made of Trilithium, the only known power source for starships. We had waited for the aliens' return for a week. Little did we know of Boccia, the Italian style of bowling, back then.

I spotted Tony sitting on the aging log that was

about as long as a park bench. Leaning my mountain bike against the closest tree, I climbed over the fallen trunk and settled down next to him. Neither of us said a word.

Gazing at the small pond for quite some time gave us the chance to silently make up. When the concert of frogs turned the evening into a romantic night, I rested my head on Tony's shoulder and let out a sigh that seemed to have been stuck in my chest since the last time he'd climbed out of my window.

His arm wrapped around my shoulders, his cheek pressed against my brow. It was like all those many times when I was in his arms before, utterly content, completely safe. But this time I felt no tingle in my gut. No butterflies. No joyful heart-pounding. Like all the excitement had faded out of me.

In a way I missed it. In another…I didn't. I knew why the feeling was lacking now. He'd hurt me on a level that was beyond repair. But somehow even that was okay. Things changed. We were growing up. And I couldn't hold it against him.

"Sorry. I didn't intend to ruin your summer by being the master of ass-land," he said in a very calm voice.

I let that apology hang in the air for a few

minutes.

Finally, I scooted out of his embrace, lifted my legs to the trunk and hugged my knees to my chest, facing him. "Why did it never happen with us? The couple thing I mean. I've spent more time in my life with you than with anyone else. We cuddled, we played, we talked. We did everything together. Why did we never kiss?" Amazing. One might think I'd knocked back half a bowl of punch to be able to babble so free from the heart and not blush one bit.

Tony rubbed the back of his neck, giving me a tight smile. "I don't know. Maybe hanging out was too normal for us." He licked his bottom lip. Swinging one leg over the log, he sat astride and grabbed both my ankles in front of him. "At least it was for me. I kind of took you for granted. Your love for me was permanent. Why would I have worried about losing you?"

Because Ryan Hunter came along while you were busy with someone else. "Yeah, why would you?"

"The thing is I never knew how much it would hurt to see you kissing another guy. You made me learn that lesson the hard way."

"You know I always wanted you to be my first." And my last for that matter. The fact I could tell him this now had me wondering how far I really had distanced myself from him, emotionally.

"That ship has sailed away, I suppose." He angled his head with that typical sheepish smile. I still loved him for that, if nothing else. Suddenly he held my ankles tighter, moved my legs apart and scooted forward. When he let go, my thighs rested on top of his. We were sitting in a very new, very *intimate* position. His face was so close I could count the lashes on his lids.

I realized he was a breath away from kissing me. And suddenly I was smiling. "You aren't really going to do this, are you?"

"Why not?" The smirk didn't totally vanish from his lips. "I think for the sake of all those years I granted you the larger part of my comforter when you fell asleep in my bed, we should at least give it a shot."

I didn't know what to say to that, so I didn't say anything at all. And then Tony broke into the last inch of my personal space and kissed me. Slowly. Sensually. Like I'd always wanted him to do. He tasted perfect. Warm, sweet, natural…everything I expected it to be. His hands covering mine were a gentle caress.

When I drew back, his warm blue eyes searched

my face. Sweet dimples appeared on his cheeks. "This is not going to happen again, is it?"

A sigh escaped me on a soft laugh. "Why do you think that?"

He brushed his knuckle along my jaw. "Because a kiss from me obviously fails to make you shiver like one look from Ryan Hunter does."

I laughed again. And this time I felt my cheeks warming slightly. Yeah, just thinking of Ryan did that to me.

Tony shifted back on the log, and I resumed my curled-up position. With my cheek resting on my knees, I watched the vanilla moon creep up above the lush crowns of the trees. Next to me, Tony fished out his phone and his fingers flew over the keypad.

"What are you doing?"

"Texting a friend." When he was done, he tucked it back into his pocket.

Minutes ticked by as we gazed at the sky together. Although peaceful and relaxed, the situation felt awkward. For both of us. Like no one knew what to say. Not something that happened very often between us. Relief swamped me when he dropped his gaze from the sky and said, "Some of the guys are going to watch *The Avengers* this weekend. Wanna come?"

I wondered who *some of the guys* were. I knew from Susan that Tony wasn't talking to Chloe anymore. But if she was with the group, I sure wouldn't go. "Maybe. Who's coming?"

"Andy, Sasha, Alex. He's with Simone now, by the way. Frederickson will come if he doesn't have to watch his baby brother. And then of course…him." He nodded his chin in the direction behind me.

That definitely gave me an electric bolt. I jerked my head around, spine straightening.

Ryan Hunter strolled toward us, hands shoved into the pockets of his jeans, the sleeves of a black shirt rolled up to the elbows. My mouth hung open at the unexpected sight of him. The pounding of my heart was so loud I was sure he could hear it. He greeted me with the tiniest tilt of his head and a slight half-smile.

"Am I disrupting something?" he asked, his eyes set on me.

"Nope. I was just about to leave."

Huh, what? My gaze snapped to Tony who'd risen from the trunk and stood next to me.

"What are you doing?" I whispered, horrified, only now realizing who he'd sent the text to.

He leaned down to speak into my ear.

"Correcting a shitload of mistakes." As he drew back, he winked. "See you later."

Oh, I should have strangled him with my bare hands. Only, I was in shock and couldn't move. Not even when Tony was gone and Ryan Hunter settled down behind me, straddling the trunk and looping his arms around my middle from behind.

His breath feathered against my neck, his muscled chest pressing against my back. "I'm sorry for what happened, but I never meant to hurt you. And I certainly didn't have any bad intentions. I swear."

"Yeah, I guess I know that. Susan told me a few interesting things today."

"Did she?" I could clearly hear how this made him a little uncomfortable, but an edge of relief filled his voice nonetheless. "So, what are we going to make of this situation?"

"Situation?" I swallowed to get rid of the dryness in my throat. "What do you mean?"

"I mean you…me…" Suddenly his lips were on my bare shoulder, brushing toward the crook of my neck. "Alone…in this place…"

His tongue trailing up my throat sent shivers along my skin. Everywhere. Down my arms, my legs. Even the hair at the back of my neck stood on end.

"With only the frogs to watch us…" He placed the softest kiss on the spot behind my ear.

My breath hitched. My mind searched for an escape from this situation. But there was none. And even if there had been, Ryan wouldn't have let me go. His hand moved up to my neck and shaped against my cheek, tilting my face slowly until I gazed into his gorgeous tiger eyes.

"What do you say, Matthews? Should we give it a try?"

I searched his face for a reason not to believe in his sincerity. The tiniest lie even. But nothing. He seemed to mean what he said. A reluctant smile tugged on my lips. "Only if you start using my first name, *Hunter.*"

He laughed at that, softly, melodiously. Beautifully. His nose skimmed across my cheekbone, and he pressed his lips gently on mine. A volcano erupted in my stomach with thousands of butterflies set free. But he wouldn't kiss me just yet. Instead he drew back, a spark lighting up his eyes. "While we're at it, *Lisa*…I have a condition, too."

"You do? What is it?"

"For the time being—" He emphasized each word. "I'll be the only one climbing through your window."

Now he made me laugh. "I think I can agree to that."

"You *think?*" Ryan nipped my bottom lip with his teeth.

The tiny, playful sting had me surrendering completely. "Okay, you win. You'll be the only one."

He thrust his hand in my hair, holding me tight against him with his other placed flat on my stomach. "See, baby, that sounds a damn lot better." He bent his head and captured my mouth. His soft breath on my cheek coated my neck and arms with goose bumps, while his tongue traced the seam of my lips, demanding entrance. My heart knocked hard against my ribcage. Ryan must have been able to feel it, because before he went on with the kiss, he whispered against my lips, "You nervous?"

Excited! "That's just all *you*," I whispered back. Then I reached around his neck, laced my fingers in his hair, and pulled him closer. I was done waiting. "Will you kiss me now or what?"

His mouth curved into a smile. I could feel that, just before he made me turn around in his arms, so I straddled his lap, and he cuddled me tight against him. With his hands first in my hair and then everywhere, he kissed me in a way that made my insides tickle. His tongue slid against mine so slowly, so tenderly, that I thought I'd die if he stopped only for a second. But Ryan Hunter didn't stop kissing me. He gave me everything I ever wanted from a boy. It had just taken me a little while to realize, I wanted it from him and no one else.

With the feeling of totally melting into him, I didn't notice how fast or slow time passed. It seemed like only a second to me, or maybe it lasted for eternity. Being enclosed in Ryan's arms, I didn't care…

Because it was perfect.

Epilogue

Ryan locked the front door of the beach house and dropped the keys back into the potted plant on the porch. The briny breeze of the sea did little to cool my heated skin. He turned to me, hooking his fingers through the belt loops of my jeans. "Come here, sexy wench."

Jeez, I loved that dangerous smile on his lips. Way too much, I decided.

His hands slowly flicked open a button on my blouse.

"What are you doing?" I grabbed his wrists. "We

just left your room. I think I have enough hickeys all over me for a day or two." He was like a wolf, marking me with his bites. But then, I enjoyed that as much as I enjoyed him pressing me against the wall now and sliding my red top down my shoulders.

"It's hot," he whispered in my ear. "And you look amazing in that bikini. I can't allow you to hide that from me." He nibbled a path down my throat.

Warm chills dusted my skin with goose bumps. "If you don't stop that, we'll be late for the movie."

"What do I care about a movie, when I have my lovely girlfriend all to myself?"

"Tony and the others are waiting." The mention of Tony's name wouldn't go down too well. I grimaced the same moment as Ryan stiffened and stopped nuzzling my neck. Yeah, that growl was to be expected. But if I didn't find a way to curb Ryan, we'd never leave the house again.

I must be out of my mind to choose *The Avengers* over *him*.

He looked at his wristwatch. "We still have an hour and a half."

"I want to shower before we go out."

"All right. But this"—he pulled the blouse down my arms—"is mine." He pressed a brief, hard kiss on my lips.

With my hand in his, he tugged me down the stairs. I loved the way he couldn't keep his hands off me. How he held me so close and cuddled with me. He never let me out of his sight. The guy sure felt a little possessive there, and he made no effort to hide that from me or anyone else. I couldn't stop myself from smiling.

He tucked my top into the back pocket of his jeans, and it hung teasingly down his backside as he bent to roll the hems of his jeans up to the middle of his calves. The stunning view made me feel hot all over. He straightened, and I quickly looked away. His eyes narrowed, a knowing smirk on his lips at the embarrassing color of heat flooding my face.

"What, Matthews? You like my butt?"

I bit my bottom lip, wanting to deny it, but why bother? I loved everything about him. For instance, his sparkling brown eyes and his mouth, when he cast me that sweet half-smile. "Yep. That and a few other things."

"So? What would that be?"

I merely smiled, taunting him for not using my name by not answering. "Didn't we agree you'd use my first name from now on?"

He quirked his brows. It came out innocently enough. "Did we?"

"I think it was one of the conditions, yeah."

"Ah, conditions, conditions." He laughed. "I should have made you swear never to wear anything other than that bikini top when you're with me."

"I doubt that's a good idea. Especially when we're at your place. You had me sweating bullets back there." I nodded over my shoulder to his parents' bungalow. The only reason he managed to drag me in there was because I insisted he leave the wide window in his room open so I could escape the moment I heard someone enter the house. I didn't want to be another girl caught with him.

"Aw, look who's still worried." He brushed a stray wisp of hair behind my ear.

Yeah right. And if he wasn't grinning so stupidly, I would have bought his compassion. I slapped his hand away. "That is your fault. You scared the crap out of me last time when your mom came in."

"I know. I felt your heart pounding like it would jump out of your chest when I had you pinned to the floor behind the couch." He paused. Mischief crept into his gaze. "Or could it be that you were just excited to be so close to me?"

"You'll never find out." I stuck my tongue out at him.

Ryan slung his arm around me, and together we walked back up the beach.

"You know," he murmured moments later, a serious note in his voice. "I met your parents this morning. I think it's time for you to meet mine."

I gulped. "What, now?"

"There's still plenty of time until the movie begins. And they should both be home right now. We could just pop in for a moment before meeting up with the others."

My heart drummed an uneasy beat. "But you haven't even told them about me yet."

"So what? You didn't tell yours before you dragged me into your kitchen to say hello."

True. That had really been mean of me. "But you're always cool with everything. I knew it wouldn't trouble you."

"And meeting my parents would be a problem for you?"

"You haven't even told me their names."

"Their names are Mom and Dad." He chuckled.

I rolled my eyes at him. "Amazing...that's what I call my parents, too."

"Yeah, popular names." His hand slid down from my shoulder. His warm palm rested on my waist just above my shorts as he pulled me to his side.

His touch on my bare skin never failed to set a bunch of butterflies loose in my belly.

"But maybe it isn't such a good idea to meet them now," he said. "They'll make us stay all evening, and we won't be able to get to the show in time."

I breathed a relieved sigh.

Ryan fished out his cell phone from the chest pocket of his shirt.

"Calling someone?" I asked.

He nodded and placed one finger on his lips, shushing me as he held the phone to his ear. "Mom? Hi. Just wanted to say we're going to have a guest for dinner tomorrow."

My chin dropped to my chest.

"Yes, a friend," he continued. "Oh, and could you please invite Rach and Phil, too?"

What in the world was he up to? Getting his entire family together to introduce me? I wanted to yank the phone out of his hand and toss it into the waves cascading over our ankles.

He paused then laughed, turning away from me. "No, Mom. If it was that, I swear I wouldn't be calling." He said goodbye and rang off. Gently, he slid his knuckle under my chin and closed my mouth. "We have a date tomorrow evening."

"Yeah, I heard that. So you're going to throw me in there like a bone in front of a wolf pack?"

"Don't worry. I'll be with you, and I'll protect you all evening. No one gets to gnaw on you." He leaned in and softly bit into my earlobe. "Apart from me, that is."

I whined, already dreading the dinner with his family. "If you liked me one bit, you wouldn't do that."

"I like you two bits, and that's exactly why we need to do this. Now stop worrying. It can't be worse than your father asking me if I knew how to use a condom."

I gasped and pulled back. "He asked you that?"

"Not exactly. He mentioned something like it to your mother when we were out of the room. Didn't you hear him whispering?"

I hadn't. "Oh my God, how embarrassing is that?"

"Calm down. Your parents are great. And your mom's blueberry muffins are amazing." He pressed a kiss to my brow, then took my hand, and pulled me forward with a smirk on his face. "But maybe you should assure your dad that I do know how to not knock you up."

I'd rather dig a tunnel from here to China and disappear.

We trudged up to the road where he'd parked his car. "Can I have my shirt back now, or do you want me to ride half-naked in your car?"

His face lit up. "You mean I have a choice?"

"No!" I laughed and reached behind him to grab my top. But it wasn't there. "Where is it?"

Ryan looked at me puzzled. Then we both pivoted and stared down the way we'd come. The good thing was we spotted my bright red top some fifty feet away. The bad thing…a wave had caught it and washed it back and forth on the beach.

I sprinted down the soft sand and grabbed the dripping wet and sandy blouse. Nothing I could wear over my bikini.

"Oh, great," I muttered, holding the mess against the chiding sun.

"It's not the end of the world, Lisa." Ryan laughed, strolling over to me. He'd started unbuttoning his shirt and slipped out of it. "You can take mine for the ride home."

He held it out to me, but I only gawked at his naked chest.

His left eyebrow tilted up. "Okay. If you don't want it…"

I jerked the shirt out of his hand before he could withdraw it and pushed my arms through the short sleeves that still reached to my elbows. The white material with a soft blue pattern felt warm on my skin. It smelled like Ryan, and I couldn't resist holding the collar to my nose and breathing in deep. The shirt was way too long for me. My hot pants were completely hidden beneath it.

As I buttoned it up, a whole new level of danger flickered in his eyes. He stepped closer and wrapped his arms around me, bringing his lips to my ear. "I like you in my clothes." His palm shaped against my cheek. With a gentle tilt he made me look into his eyes. "You're way too sexy for your own good, Matthews."

He captured my lips and kissed me deeply. I stood on my tiptoes to match his size—well, tried to, but no chance. He yanked me against him. I felt each of his hard muscles underneath his skin. Boy, I could never get enough of him. He only had to give my bottom lip this playful nip and I was ready to surrender. The rest of the world faded from my mind.

When Ryan started to ease the kiss, I only became more eager. I got a hold of his hair and held him in place, making sure he wouldn't stop kissing me. Not yet. For a moment he responded with a sensual slide of his tongue against mine. But then he drew back. "You know we have to get you home so you can shower, and if I remember it right, we're supposed to watch a movie."

I brushed my fingertips over his whiskered cheek. "What do I care about a movie, if I have my gorgeous boyfriend all to myself?"

He dipped his head back and laughed. "Yeah, right. And afterward you'll make me pay for making us late. No way. Get your butt into my car, Matthews. *Now*."

I made a pouty face, but didn't protest when he walked me to the street. In fact, I did want to see that film, because Tony would be there, and I hadn't seen him since the evening he left me alone in the woods with Ryan. I really needed to know if we were all right.

We put our shoes on, which we'd left behind in the car, then Ryan drove us to my house. I darted through the door first. Since he wasn't wearing a shirt,

I hoped I could sneak him past the kitchen without my parents seeing him. Good, the kitchen was empty. But when we headed for the stairs, my dad came out of the living room and stopped dead in the threshold. His scowl deepened and zeroed in on Ryan.

Before my dad got a chance to say anything, Ryan held out my sandy, still-soaking top. "Wet blouse," he said quickly. "She needed something to wear."

My mother came up behind my dad and rubbed his upper arm, laughing. "I told you he's a gentleman, darling." She winked at me and smiled at Ryan.

I felt the warm caress of victory. My mom loved my boyfriend, and she'd see to relaxing my dad around him, too.

"Thank you," I mouthed to her, then I ushered Ryan up the stairs.

I hurried through my shower then dressed in jeans and a gray sweatshirt with Mickey Mouse on the front. To my disappointment, Ryan had put on his shirt again. But I'd done enough drooling for a day anyway, and it was getting late. We needed to hurry to meet the others before the movie started.

In front of the show, I caught a glimpse of Frederickson chatting with Alex and Simone. Andy and Sasha waited in the queue in front of the ticket counter. Ryan joined them, leaving me with the others.

"Hi." I waved to all of them.

Simone beamed at me, her hand tight in Alex's. They made a nice couple.

I got a little anxious when I couldn't see Tony anywhere. He wouldn't have changed his mind last minute because of my being with Ryan, would he? I really hoped not.

"Where's Tony? Isn't he coming?"

"Er…he is." Simone's amused gaze moved to a spot behind my shoulder.

"Looking for someone, Liz?" Tony's breath ruffled my hair.

I jerked around, unable to hide my grin.

"Just found him." For a heartbeat, I felt the need to hug him, but I thought better of it and shoved my hands into my pockets. "It's good to see you," I kept my voice low, so only he would hear.

He smiled. His blue eyes flashed in a teasing manner, like the Tony I used to know. "You look great tonight. Happy."

I nodded, accepting his compliment. It felt good to see that we still were what we'd always been…comfortable with each other.

From behind, fingers slipped under the waistband of my jeans, and I was pulled a tiny step backward. Ryan gazed down at me with the slightest hint of insecurity in his eyes. I took his hand and squeezed. Longing and a smile replaced his insecurity.

He gave Tony a knuckle pound. "Hey, Mitchell. Are we cool?"

"Of course," Tony replied.

I drew in a deep, relieved breath. This would be a perfect evening. Everything was all right. What more could I wish for?

When our small group headed inside, Ryan held me back for another moment. I turned to him. "What's wrong?"

"What did Mitchell say to you?" He didn't look annoyed or worried. Just curious.

"He asked me if I was happy."

He waited a second, touching his brow to mine. "Are you?"

I loved how easily I could lose myself in his beautiful tiger eyes. I pressed a soft kiss to his cheek and whispered into his ear, "Absolutely."

If you fell in love with Lisa and Ryan, watch out for the next installment in the *Grover Beach Players* series and let Ryan Hunter tell you from his perspective how he landed Lisa.

There are two sides to every story.
Mine's the one with the bad decisions—and the best intentions.

Yeah, I've kissed more girls in high school than I can count. Doesn't matter. Because the only one I've ever wanted is too busy mooning over my best friend.

Watching Lisa Matthews worship Tony has been slow torture for years. Then this summer, genius-boy hooks up with someone else... and asks me to keep her distracted. Game on.

Step one: get her on my soccer team.
Step two: get her into my orbit.
Step three: get under her skin in all the right ways.

She calls me an insufferable playboy, which is adorable, because she has no clue what I'm like when I'm actually going after someone.
One-on-one soccer training should fix that.

The tequila kiss afterward?
Not planned. Not smart.
But the best mistake I ever made.

Ryan Hunter
ANNA KATMORE

A few guys stood around the pool table. Justin was playing a game against Alex when I came into the room adjoining the main hall. Justin looked up and his face crumpled worse than a raisin. "Ah man, sorry, that wasn't my intention," he apologized again, straightening and leaning on his cue.

"Forget it." I grinned. "It's all set for Monday."

That made him lift his brows in an impressed way and nod.

"What's set for Monday?" Alex demanded after he shot the yellow ball into a hole. "And what wasn't your intention, Juz?"

"Nothing," Justin and I shot back at him.

"Is there money in the pot?" I tried to change the topic as I sat down on the couch between Frederickson and a guy whose real name I didn't know but who we all called Sylvester.

Alex tapped the stack of dollar bills on the table

with the tip of his cue. "Twenty-five from each."

"I'll play the winner." I didn't have to play for money to stock up my bank account, but it was way more fun playing with the guys if *they* had the right incentive. For one, they didn't play pool like sissies then.

It wasn't easy to tell who was the better player, but this time Justin came out the winner, because Alex sank the eight ball early.

"Fifty's in the pot," Justin said to me with a wide sneer. "I want to see your money if you want to play."

I pulled two twenties and a ten from my wallet and placed them on Justin's prize money. "I'm in."

Alex passed me the cue, and I chalked it while someone else racked the balls for us. Because I'd only just come in, I got to shoot first. Number twelve ended in the left corner pocket, which left Justin with solids and me with stripes. It was a fast game. In only four turns I had dumped most of my balls. Only the orange and white ball—number thirteen—was left, and I holed it into a corner pocket with a spectacular shot over three cushions. Now just the eight ball, and victory would be mine.

My confident smirk at Justin made the guy a little nervous. "Come on, Ryan, give a friend a chance. You can't hole the ball just yet," he whined.

That didn't irritate me. "What's your problem, Justin? Afraid your mama's going to find out you're playing for money?" I leaned forward, focusing on the black ball, measuring my final shot.

"My mama doesn't give a damn. But I *really, really* need this *Spiderman* comic. It's an original."

Ah, right. With Justin, if it wasn't about BMX or girls, it was always comics. He hoarded them like squirrels hoarded nuts, and I couldn't believe how much he was willing to spend on those books when his pocket money for a year was what I got in a month.

He had me feeling bad for him…almost. Heck, this was a guy thing, and I couldn't lose just to make a friend happy. When you're eighteen, it's all about rep.

I positioned the cue in a perfect line with the white ball, the eight, and the left corner pocket. I was so close to winning this game. Only, I made the mistake of looking up for a second and froze.

For an immeasurable moment, I forgot to breathe. How dare she come in here and ruin this game for me? Ah *God*, how dare she look so good? It only took a second for the others to realize something had gone wrong, and they all turned to find my personal downfall standing in the doorway.

Lisa grimaced and played uncomfortably with the hem of her top. "Is something wrong?"

Everything was wrong. It always was with me when this girl was anywhere near. The day I had first seen Lisa Matthews, I'd tripped over the soccer ball and landed face first in the dirt. She always made me forget about anything else around me. And now, she'd cost me a fair sum if she didn't turn around and walk out so I could get my head back in the game.

No such luck. Justin made sure of that. He rushed to her side, the grin of victory sitting fat on his face. "You just saved my life, hun."

Lisa seemed a little surprised when Justin laid his arm around her shoulders and pulled her farther into the room where the warm light from above played up the various shades of brown in her hair. I wanted to kick my best friend's ass at this moment because, for one, he knew I'd screw up with Lisa in the room and he was using that to his advantage. And secondly, because he dared to lay his fucking arm around my girl. He was going to pay for *both* later.

"Ah…yes," Lisa said and looked from Justin to me. "And how so?"

She had *no* idea. That was one of the things I

liked about her most—that she was always so sweetly unaware of everything. Especially of the crap that was just about to fall on my head.

"He can't play when someone is watching him," Justin stated the obvious. "Totally screws up then."

Her brows knitted together. "But you *all* are watching him."

The way she spoke to everybody else but looked only at me made me grin.

"Yeah, but we're not girls." That was Alex from the back of the room, and he certainly enjoyed selling me out. Bastards. Were they all against me tonight?

It was probably time to say something in my defense, to save my honor, but all I did was fix Lisa with a salacious stare as I straightened and chalked the tip of my cue.

"Sorry," she croaked. "I'll leave you guys alone then."

Justin didn't let her slip away. "Uh-uh, no way, hun! You're my insurance of getting that comic book. You stay."

His arm around her got mightily on my nerves, even though he made Lisa smile. And heck, she had the prettiest smile in all of Grover Beach. One that conjured sweet dimples on her cheeks and made her pretty green eyes crinkle. One that made me lick my bottom lip, wanting nothing more than to kiss her.

And because she was still only gazing at me and no one else as she smiled, I couldn't help that one corner of my mouth tilted up. I was in serious trouble. Lisa distracted me something awful. She made me lose my mind and she was about to make me lose this game, too. More importantly, she'd made me lose face in front of my closest friends—and yet she still lived. *Damn, I must be in love with this girl.*

Taking a deep breath, I shook my head and leaned over the table once more. Everybody was tense and silent. They would've just loved to see me butcher this shot. I cleared my throat, playing for more time, hoping for a miracle that would swipe Lisa out of the room this second. But she remained, and I couldn't stop looking at her. Hard as I tried to concentrate on the balls in front of me, my gaze drifted up to her face time and time again.

Ah, to hell with it! This game was lost.

I dropped my forehead to the edge of the table and laughed. "Take your money, Andrews. I give up."

The boys broke out in a rowdy cheer. *Yeah, right, rub it in guys!*

Bracing my palms on the pool table, I hung my

head for a moment, accepting their gloating. But when I looked up, Lisa was still there capturing me with her gaze, and I knew it was totally worth it.

"I'm so sorry," she mouthed.

And she'd better be. Lisa probably had no idea how badly she'd damaged my rep and that the boys would never let me live this down. But I wasn't angry. How could I be? She was the sweetest distraction that had ever walked through my door.

I didn't let her out of my sight but smirked and mouthed back, "*You* are banned from this room."

She didn't move an inch when I slowly walked around the table toward her. In fact, she even pressed a little harder against the wall, her eyes growing wider, her breathing coming just a bit faster. It looked like she couldn't make up her mind whether she should shy away from me or be fascinated.

I stood only half a foot away from her, with the cue tight in one hand. The other I placed against the wall next to her head so she couldn't escape me. "You just cost me fifty bucks."

"Yeah, I know. But he *really, really* needs this comic book." She batted her long lashes at me. To my shame, I had to admit that this simple move bulldozed right through my coolness.

I laughed. "Siding with the enemy. I should have known." Then I seized the opportunity to touch her one more time tonight and placed my hand in the small of her back. "For tonight, this room is off limits for you." Gently, I pushed her through the door back into the main hall and enjoyed every second my hand lay on her warm body.

"Oh why? It's so much fun to watch you…screw up."

She mockingly glanced up at me, and I should have bitten her bottom lip for that impish pout.

But I resisted that urge and also the one to brush my thumb over her lip. Instead, I leaned in a little closer. "Off you go."

She obeyed, and I didn't know if that made me happy or sad. But as soon as she was gone, I closed the sliding wood door and slumped with my back against it, facing a hoard of sneering guys.

"Can anybody tell me why I never have my phone ready to record when things like that happen?" Chris Donovan popped open a new bottle of beer and saluted into the room. "Hunter screwing up a game because of Lisa Matthews. This is priceless."

"Mitchell is so going to kill you for stealing his girl," Alex said while rearranging the balls on the green felt.

"Mitchell doesn't have to know," I sneered back. "Anyway, I'm not stealing her. That was just some harmless flirting. Nothing to blow a fuse about."

"What *she* did was harmless. What *you* did, man, was begging on your knees to get laid."

A laugh escaped me at the honesty and probable truth in that. "Fuck you, Winter. Are we playing pool now or what?"

"You just epically failed. I'm not playing *you*, Hunter." He cast me a mocking glare then turned around. "Frederickson, get your ass off the couch. We're playing."

I shoved his shoulder for that last remark, and Alex laughed as he grabbed the edge of the pool table for balance.

Donovan hoisted himself onto the mini-bar, feet dangling, and leaned forward to rest his elbows on his thighs. The fat silver chain around his neck slipped out from under the collar of his T-shirt and swayed back and forth. "I never knew you felt anything for the chick."

Jeez, I'd have preferred if we didn't discuss my feelings and just continued with a nice evening of playing pool. "I'm not saying I do."

"Right, that's what you have us for," Alex said, still struggling to stop laughing. "And, dude, you got it bad."

As if I didn't know that. When I cut a glance over to Justin, the only one in the room who had known from the start how I felt, he shrugged, clearly telling me that I had no choice but to face it with the guys.

Frederickson got to his feet, grabbed my cue, and placed a hand on my shoulder. "Sincere condolences, Hunter. That girl won't let you get within a yard of her."

Rubbing the back of my neck, I couldn't bite down a smirk. "I believe I was way closer than that just a couple of minutes ago."

"Oooh," a collective taunting echoed through the room. I hated it when the guys behaved like some silly chicks at a bachelorette party. But at eighteen, almost everything was worth making a fool of oneself. I'd totally be with them if the joke wasn't on me tonight.

I dropped to the couch and leaned my head on the back, dragging my hands over my face, mostly to cover my stupid grin. "Shut up, you fuckers."

Alex made tsking noises before his first shot, knocking the balls in all directions. "Language, dude." When none of the balls dropped into a pocket, he dumped his ass next to me and waited for Frederickson to take his shot. His long legs stretched out and crossed at the ankles, he cast me a sideways glance. "Seriously, you think you stand a chance with the chick? To me it looks like she's happy to be Mitchell's groupie forever."

At this point, I wasn't sure if determination and charm alone were enough to change Lisa's mind, but I was ready to die trying. By what she'd showed me tonight, she wasn't totally resistant to everything I said or did. Maybe the problem was just that she'd never considered a different future for herself than one with Anthony Mitchell's ring on her finger. But there were so many possibilities for her, if only she would open up. And I was definitely one of them.

"That's because she doesn't know what she's going to miss while running after him," I said to Alex.

"You're going to show her?"

"Yeah. Hunter's just the man for that," Chris pointed out with an impish waggling of his brows. "I bet he has her in his bed before the week's over."

"Twenty that she doesn't even let him kiss her in that time," Frederickson countered.

"Guys!" I shouted to get their attention then nailed them all with a severe stare. "Don't you even *think* of making a wager on this. Matthews isn't a girl you fool around with to win a bet. First, because she's the friend of a friend. And second—" I paused then slowly lifted one corner of my mouth. "Because I would hate to see you lose your money, Frederickson."

That made the guys hoot and whistle, and they all wished me luck. I definitely needed it if I wanted to land Lisa.

A few minutes passed before everyone was cool again, and we could play pool for a little while without distraction. When we'd depleted the mini-bar down to just tonic water, I left the guys to grab some drinks. "Going to get beer. Anybody else want one?"

Alex said yes, and Justin ordered soda.

As I walked into the kitchen, my hands immediately fisted by my sides, and I had trouble unclenching my teeth. Lisa sat on the counter, and Mitchell stood between her dangling feet. At first look I thought they were kissing, and my heart hurt so bad that I wondered if someone should call an ambulance because I was suffering a cardiac arrest. Until I realized Chloe was with them and Lisa was apparently having some trouble sitting upright. I'd sent her off with Sprite. How the hell had she ended up drunk?

Chloe pulled on Mitchell's arm, but he didn't seem to be ready to go. "Anthony, you promised to dance with me," she nagged him.

And then, in spite of my rage over Tony standing so close to Lisa, I had to suppress a chuckle as Lisa iterated in the voice of a preschooler, *"Anthony, you promised to dance with me."*

That sure pissed Chloe off. "What's wrong with *her?*"

"She just had a little too much of the punch," said Tony. "I'll be with you in a minute."

I was about to tell him he should go with her now and let me handle Lisa. In her condition, it wasn't a good idea to let her deal with Chloe and the crap she didn't know about them yet.

But at the same moment, Lisa's head dipped to his shoulder. "I'm so tired. Can we go home?" she whined.

Chloe took a step back and folded her arms over her chest, which threatened to jump out of her plastered-on black dress. "Aw, come on, Anthony. You're not going to leave already. It's only eleven. Take her upstairs to one of Hunter's guest rooms. She can sleep there."

Oh no.

"And not bother you any longer?" A moan came from Lisa who looked like she was already falling asleep on Tony's shoulder.

Not up to getting involved in the drama of the night, I walked up beside Mitchell and said, "You don't want to do that. In her state, she's not safe in any of the guest rooms. You know how the parties go on the later it gets." So what option did we have left? "Take her to my room."

"*What?*" Lisa and Tony shouted, Lisa suddenly sitting up straight with her eyes wide open. So much for getting her in my bed before the week was over.

"Don't be ridiculous, guys." I rolled my eyes as if the thought of doing anything with Lisa was totally absurd. If they knew the truth, Tony wouldn't trust me one bit. "She'll be awake and gone before I even get upstairs." Unfortunately, that was also the truth.

Since Lisa was as drunk as a rum truffle, it was up to Mitchell to decide for her. He was, after all, her best friend and therefore responsible...somehow. But he hesitated.

"Hell, do it already, Anthony, and come back fast," Chloe demanded.

When Tony pressed his lips into a straight line, I thought he would never agree. But then he said,

"Come on, Liz," and pulled her off the counter. With his arm around her waist, he steadied her and walked her to the door.

After only three steps, she slipped away from him and knocked against the fridge, bounced back, and stumbled. "Pardon me," she said as if the fridge had just grown a soul.

She was going to run into the counter next, so I wrapped my arms around her, pulling her tight against me. "Didn't I tell you to stay away from the strawberries?" I growled into her ear, immediately getting high on her beautiful scent.

"Strawberries? There was one in my last soda." The silly girl grinned like a loon. "It was yummy."

"Yummy, all right." I chuckled. Then I scooped her up. Lord, had I known that this was Heaven, I'd have tried to be a nicer guy in the past. Her body was light and soft, and her warmth seeped through my shirt, causing my skin to prickle. My hands lay on places that I wouldn't have dared to dream of touching just a couple of days ago.

"I'll carry her to my room, Mitchell. You can grab her when you go. Or come back for her in the morning." Or…don't come back at all and just leave her with me.

"You sure?" Yep, he didn't trust me at all.

"Yes. Go dance with Chloe or she'll pester me next."

He looked at Summers, and she flashed a radiant grin at him. All right! The battle was won. Mitchell handed Lisa into my care. If she'd been *my* best friend, I wouldn't have done that.

Savoring every second of cuddling Lisa to my chest, I carried her upstairs. She wrapped her arms around my neck, and suddenly her head rested on my shoulder. I briefly closed my eyes and my jaw tightened as I struggled to stay cool.

"You don't like dancing with Chloe?" she murmured.

I touched my cheek to her brow. "Would you?"

"I don't like her, period."

That was obvious. "And I know exactly why that is."

"Really?"

I just wanted to tell her that everybody knew how she was in love with my buddy, but she distracted me when her nose brushed against my neck and she inhaled deeply. "You smell good," she said in her lovely, drunken ramble, and I knew that without the strawberries I would have never heard this from her lips.

It made me happy and I laughed, and though I would have loved to get her into a conversation where she could tell me all the other things she might like about me, I knew it was wrong, because she would hate me for it tomorrow. If she even remembered it then. "Time to go to bed, Matthews."

Opening the door to my room with Lisa in my arms wasn't an easy thing, but I managed it with my elbow and carried her over to my wide bed underneath the window. Before I laid her down, I hugged her a little tighter with the intention that whatever else happened, I'd always remember this wonderful moment where I held the girl I'd loved for years for the very first time.

When she snuggled up to my pillow and sniffed like she couldn't get enough of the scent on it, I smiled to myself. Then I pulled her shoes off, covered her bare legs with the quilt, and squatted down beside her, staring at her sweet, pale face. "You comfortable?"

Her eyes were closed as she made a whiny face. "I'm not sure. But can you check if my head has sprouted helicopter blades?"

I stroked her soft, straight hair, brushing the long bangs from her forehead. "No helicopter blades, baby," I whispered so low that she couldn't hear. A little louder I said, "That will go away when you sleep. If you need anything, the light switch is right in front of your nose and the bathroom is the next door on the left."

She didn't reply or move. I was afraid she'd already fallen asleep without hearing the most important information when one was drunk and sick. As much as I adored this girl, I'd rather she didn't throw up in my bed. "Did you hear me?"

Her mouth curved into a strained grin. "Light, nose. Toilet, left. Gotcha." She even gave me a thumbs-up, which reassured me.

I rose from the floor, but just when I went to walk away, she said my name. "Hunter?"

Hunkering down again, I leaned my forearms on the mattress. "Hm?"

She dragged a deep sigh. "Sorry about the pool game."

Yeah, I know you are. But I'm not. The way our gazes had met across that table was special. Way too intimate to be brushed off as harmless flirting. I let my glance move around me, scanning the familiar things in my room, then I looked back at her, the one thing that was totally unfamiliar in here. She made everything complete for me.

Gently, so as not to wake her up again, I stroked her warm cheek with the back of my fingers. "Sleep tight, princess."

More books by Anna Katmore

ON THIN ICE
Counting Fireflies
Splintered North
*

Seventeen Butterflies

GROVER BEACH PLAYERS
Play With Me
Ryan Hunter
T Is For…
Dating Trouble
The Trouble with Dating Sue
*

The Impossible Bet
This Kitten Has Claws

CRUSHED HEARTS
Unfair Love
Broken Dawn
Awaking Trust

DREAMS OF NEVER EVER
Neverland
Pan's Revenge

WHISPERING PAGES
No Prince for Riding Hood
A Wolf in her Way

*

Eloyn
My Secret Vampire
You were my Fairytale
Three Shades of Sinful

"I write stories because I can't breathe without."

Anna Katmore lives in an enchanting world of her own. It's a place where logic waits patiently at the gate and only dreamers are allowed to enter. Beware, though, once you step through, you may never wish to leave again.

Disney isn't just her passion; it's her attitude toward life. If she could, she'd wrap the world in a little stardust and save it from itself. Her patronus is a wolf. Her wand is a broken twig from an apple tree, 13¾ inches long, yet full of charm. And although there's always glitter on her shoes, she keeps a safe distance from Cinderella's glass slippers. Too risky, something might break.

For more magic, visit www.annakatmore.com